Black Is The Colour

Revenge Is Always An Act of Passion

Seamus Connolly

First Published © 2022 Seamus Connolly
Re Published in 2022 by SPellBound Books.
Copyright © Seamus Connolly

PRINT ISBN:-

Cover Art © a r t E A S T c r e a t i v e 2021

For Carol Ann, Cara-Marie, Ciaran-Patrick.

And my Parents - for everything.

Black is the colour of my true love's hair,
Her lips are like some roses fair,
She's the sweetest smile, And the gentlest hands,
I love the ground, Whereon she stands.
I go to the Clyde and I mourn and weep,
satisfied, I ne'er can be,
I write her a letter, just a few short lines,
And suffer death, a thousand times.

Scottish Folk Song

The Gorbals, Glasgow, 1962

'It's freezing. How far's it tae yer house?'

'No long, jist 'bout twenty minutes' walk.'

'Whit, in heels and a bloody mini skirt?'

'Check her legs, Eddie, they're turning blue.'

'Does yer pal ever stop moaning Sandra?'

'Can ye no get a taxi? Thought you were the new bigshot aboot here. Have ye got drink in the house?'

'Loadsa drink. I'm celebrating, mind. It's some night, nice 'n' fresh. We'll be there soon.'

'Get a taxi flagged or I'm going hame.'

'How much are taxis these days?'

'Don't worry, I'll get it. Watch.'

'Awright, mate. Lovely evening, eh? You had a good night?'

'What you wanting?'

'Nae need tae growl, auld man, Ah'm just being friendly. You had a skin full the night?'

'A few.'

'Ye couldnae lend me a couple of pound, could ye? See Ah've got this *lassie over there and Ah need to get her in a taxi and up the road, or she'll bomb me oot. Ye know me – Jimmy Quinn's boy.'*

'You want a couple of pound ... for a taxi? Have you noticed I'm standing at a bus stop, you fucking clown? Does it look like I've a spare couple o' quid? What you say – Jimmy Quinn's son? Tell him from me he's a thug and one of life's fucking wasters.'

'Ye really don't have much manners about ye, do ye, auld yin?'

'C'mon, bro. Just leave him. He's steaming.'

'Ye see whit's inside ma coat, auld man? Now, cause Ah'm nice, you hand over whit wis asked and Ah'll ignore the fact yer disrespecting ma da.'

'Leave him mate, calm yerself doon.'

'Look, the auld fucker's legged it. Keep walking wi' they two – I'll catch ye up.'

Chapter One

Paisley, 1984

T HE SMEARED GLASS REVERBERATED as he pulled on the rusted handle. Clearing the grime from the window, he scrutinised the office. It looked like the place had been abandoned in a hurry. Files lay strewn on a frayed carpet, cabinets were open and, tellingly, a bottle of Jameson was nestled at the base of an employee's desk. That will have to change, he thought, though good taste in whiskey can't be sniffed at.

He studied the grey outer facade of the terraced buildings that climbed the steep hill of West Brae. Fresh scents filled the autumn air emanating from the rich vegetation of Oakshaw that swept westward and clashed with the harsh urban face of the Wellmeadow.

Today had been twenty years in the making. What he had committed himself to would not only shape his future but also put to bed the demons of the past.

'Thur no' in. We watch the place fur thum, security 'n' that,' a child's voice announced, the native West of Scotland brogue rolling in the rushed words. He turned swiftly to find two boys perched on the roof of his prized, jet-black BMW 3-Series car.

He had saved long and hard to acquire the German classic. He was inanely compulsive about two things: the car and his sharp appearance.

Soon other matters would occupy his time.

He frowned to express his displeasure; that and his impressive six-foot, two-inch muscular frame should be sufficient to make them reconsider their seating arrangements.

'Just in case the junkies break in,' advised the smaller of the two, his left foot, encased in a torn trainer, swinging repeatedly and connecting with the gleaming rear passenger window with each reverse movement.

'Get off the car, please.' The accent was not one that they were familiar with. Politely spoken, it carried a tone of authority and an assertiveness that assured listeners paid attention.

'Apologies,' the chubbier boy replied. Simultaneously, they jumped down and landed at his feet. 'They'll no' be back tae two, twelve tae two,' he added, steadying himself. His sharp blue eyes darted to capture every feature of the visitor.

'Tell them,' the man paused and rubbed his smoothly shaved chin. 'Sorry, inform your *client* that I will return tomorrow morning, 8:30am.'

'Yer no' fae here, are ye?' the smaller boy enquired, pushing away the light-brown hair that covered the upper part of his face. He had a look of innocence, with oval brown eyes and a cuteness that no doubt managed to get him out of trouble or punishment.

'Why aren't you two in school? Closed?'

'Aye, shut,' retorted the other boy, who looked like someone who frequently played truant from physical education lessons.

'Teachers are oan strike again. Terrible.'

'Please, pass on the message,' the visitor reiterated, moving towards the car and wiping its roof to register his displeasure.

'Err, scuse me, big man, but that sort of message could easily get forgotten or mis ... misinterrupted,' replied the more presumptuous boy. He nodded and smirked at his partner as he stretched out an open palm towards his potential client. 'Name?'

The stranger looked despairingly at the outstretched, oil-covered hand positioned under his chin, ominously close to his immaculate cream silk tie and bleach-white shirt.'

'Apologies, we also dae scrap. It's a good year fur lead 'n' copper,' the boy added, quickly substituting one filthy hand for another while pushing a frayed pilot jacket sleeve up towards his elbow.

'Tell them, tell them...' the man said as he slowly counted coins that he'd removed from his dapper suit trouser pocket '...their new boss, Cal Lynch, will be here to start work tomorrow morning.'

He slipped into the driver's seat pausing prior to closing the door sensing four eyes straining to view the plush, bespoke interior. 'Misinterpreted.'

'Whit?'

'The word you were looking for was mis-in-ter-preted.'

The roar of the precision engine reverberated between the tall sandstone buildings, the decibels competing for attention, as the wind directed the sound towards the steep West Brae.

'Bye, boys.'

'Whit was that aw about?' asked the younger boy, locking eyes with his companion.

'Not a clue, Shada. Aw' Ah know is we're a pound up. Fancy going up tae Leisureland for a game a' pool?' he smirked and placed his arm across his friend's shoulders.

Cal Lynch had anticipated starting work that afternoon. If he were honest, though, he was apprehensive as to whether it would work out as he had so assiduously planned. He wasn't in complete control of the outcome and that unnerved him. But he was determined to see this through. He had waited long enough; one more day wouldn't stretch his patience.

Chapter Two

'WHERE'S YER MAAAAMMY ...GUAN' tae baths?'

'Where's yer Maaaammy ... gaun' tae baths?'

'Where's yer Maaa...'

'Swimmer! Swimmer! Ah'm trying tae concentrate here, kid. This is stressful work, son!'

Swimmer was confused. Dixie Clark was standing rigidly, studying the exterior of the detached blonde sandstone house on Calside Avenue, an affluent residential development situated on one of the main routes heading towards Paisley town centre.

Replicating the older man's stance, Swimmer swivelled his large frame to face the Victorian property. His left hand was in his jacket pocket, firmly locking a rolled-up bath towel under his arm, while he captured the outline of the house between his thumb and forefinger of his right hand, copying the man next to him.

Dixie stood transfixed in his scrutiny of the property. His lowered eyebrows stretched his lined forehead as the sun rose brightly over the grey pitched roofs. A cacophony of noise from blackbirds in the mature mixed woodland nearby heralded a new day.

Swimmer's mind wandered to the artists he'd observed on the

4

banks of the Clyde while on trips to the People's Palace in Glasgow Green with his day centre. He was always amazed at their concentration and mesmerised by the rich autumn colours they captured on their artworks. His carer, Tom, now opted for an alternative route on their walks because of the inordinate length of time he'd had to stand shivering in the cold waiting for Swimmer's trance to be broken. Being habitually lazy, Tom preferred to take his client to the pictures where he could sit and stuff his face with popcorn at his employer's expense.

Adam Christie was his Sunday name, though everyone referred to him as Swimmer. His learning disabilities apparently stemmed from an overenthusiastic paediatrician applying forceps' during Swimmer's birth; he had done irreparable damage.

Everyone loved his warm personality and he was seldom teased about his condition. He showed a sincere, humble interest in whoever he engaged with on his travels, a warmth that radiated naturally from his personality. That, and the fact his mother could take care of most of the male inhabitants in the town with her fists as well as her sharp tongue, ensured his popularity was unquestioned.

While the artists on the banks of the Clyde, with their bright pastels, bold grey lines, and a multitude of brushes, which magically led to colours exploding and shaping a story on the sterile white canvas, were fascinating, Calside Avenue was fast losing its appeal. Swimmer's interest began to recede and, though maintaining his adopted stance, he found examining the inside of his nose with his forefinger more interesting.

'I don't get it, Swimmer,' Dixie sighed, circling his acquaintance while continuing to fix his gaze on the property. 'Dae ye see a problem wae that door?'

'Don't know, Mr Clark. I like this door,' he replied, wiping his hand on his brown, worn corduroy trousers.

'You off tae Storrie Street baths, then?'

'No, Mr Clark, no' been tae swimming baths. Mam says they're dirty and me would take too long to dry 'n' then Ah would want to go to

Allen's for chips 'n' everything on the way home, and she's ... she's fucking skint, Mam says.'

'But why the...' whispered Dixie, glancing at the rolled-up towel. 'Forget it. Listen, if yer not going swimming, ye could help me today. I'll pay ye, help yer ma? Seeing she's pratted.'

'Don't know, Mr Clark. Would need to ask Mam.'

'Don't worry about her. Me and yer ma have known each other for years, son. Call me Dixie. All ma friends dae,' he said, extending a paint-stained, callused hand. 'Welcome to the team – Dixie Clark 'n' Swimmer Christie take oan the world!'

'Right, Swimmer,' he continued, placing his hand under his conscripted companion's elbow while slowly edging him towards the ornate door. 'This wummin who stays here, Mrs Fitzgerald, dae ye know her? Doesn't matter. Anyway this wummin doesn't like the colour of the door, *and*,' he exclaimed, shaking Swimmer to life, '*and* she is paying me ... sorry, *us* tae repaint it. First thing first, though, it needs stripped. All this bright green gloss has tae come aff it and the wood sanded down. Could you help me do that, Swimmer boy?'

'Yes, Mr Clark. I like this door.'

'I agree, kid. It's a lovely door but work's work, eh? You wait here and I'll get our gear from the van.' He smiled warmly at his new friend, revealing yellow-stained teeth protruding through chapped lips, the victims of his twenty-a-day habit of Capstan Full Strength cigarettes.

Dixie returned hurriedly with a gas canister, hose and blowtorch. 'Right, Swimmer, this is what we're gonnae dae. I'll stick these goggles on ye for protection and you slip these gloves on. There ye go. Happy days, pal.'

Dixie Clark moved quickly to set up the blowtorch while constantly stretching his neck to view the pedestrians and vehicles commuting to and from the busy town. 'Right Swimmer, this is whit we'll dae. I'll light the torch and you...'

'Mr Clark!' Swimmer exclaimed, clutching his towel worriedly.

'Don't stress with that, kid. There, I'll put it on the wall next to the window.' Dixie took the opportunity to peer in the gleaming bay window to seek reassurance that the house was definitely vacant.

'Once Ah light this,' he advised, holding the lance in his partner's line of vision, 'you just go up and down, up and down, till ye see the paint bubbling, and then dae the next patch, okay?'

The panelled green door was in keeping with the pristine condition of the cottage and the well-heeled row of properties that were admired by many. Dixie had carried out work for Mrs Fitzgerald before, painting the eaves, windows, cast-iron gutters and downpipes over the past three months, as well as refurbishing sections of the interior.

The business was coming along nicely. A natural ability and practical skills in general maintenance built up over the past twenty years had come in handy when the Ferguslie Mill closed two years previously, with all 800 workers made redundant and the factory mothballed.

For two decades Dixie's employment was as a fitter's mate, ensuring the production lines, lathes and pullies remained operational and downtime was kept to a minimum. However, he rarely fixed a machine or assisted in their repair. He had cleverly entered into a mutually beneficial arrangement with his managers which allowed him to be absent from the factory while carrying out improvements to his bosses' plush villas located throughout the town. His early starts were spent not in the dusty confines of a cold, damp, and incessantly noisy factory floor but in the ornate surroundings of Paisley's Balgonie Drive or the salubrious Low Road in Castlehead, repairing sash windows or installing expensive doors.

His bosses felt an additional sense of superiority with each request. Their unrelinquished power over the workforce ensured that not only were the fitter's shifts covered in his absence but silence safeguarded his off-site activities.

Dixie enjoyed the freedom the arrangement gave him. It also allowed him to smirk at the miserable gaffers and their willingness to hold power over the workers by charging inflated prices for any materials he purchased. Not enough to cause alarm with the penny pinchers, just a bonus to supplement his weekly wage from the mill.

'Right, kiddo, you ready? Once Ah light this, you get started. I'll nip doon tae the merchants for some wire wool and undercoat. Ah might even get us some cakes oot a' the bakers, eh?'

The blue flame startled Swimmer.

'On ye go, Swims, it's nae bother. Told ye.' Dixie observed his enlisted employee start the task and reassuringly patted his broad shoulders. The paint dripped rapidly, staining the granite doorstep as Swimmer enthusiastically went to work, blistering and scorching the immaculate panelled door.

Dixie Clark could barely contain himself as he howled with laughter while surveying the scene from the safety of his van parked on the brow of the hill, far enough away not to arouse suspicion of his involvement. Swimmer was scarcely recognisable amid a plume of dark-green smoke, which had now completely enveloped his large frame and was rising and contrasting with the translucent clouds.

That old miserable cow Fitzgerald had lorded it over Dixie on many an occasion when her husband, Manny, sent him to carry out work. Now things had changed. Manny had absconded with a younger model to a factory in Stockport and, as the mill was defunct, she now had to pay for his services. The dispute had gone on long enough; she could use the two hundred pounds she owed him, but had declined to pay, to buy herself a new door.

Chapter Three

PUSHING HER HANDS INTO the deep pockets of her duffel coat, she instinctively located the volume control of her Walkman. Raising the sound to its maximum allowed The Smiths to not only dominate her thinking but also fill the vacuum in her upturned hood. *Time to switch off*, she thought.

From her induction visit she recalled that the journey from the stairs at Hawk Road to the red-brick façade and the doors of Saint Saviour High School, Paisley, would be complete in less than five minutes. She would be the new girl, the stranger in the fourth year; everyone else would be established, their idiosyncrasies well known and faults tolerated somewhat. Hopefully the girls would be friendly; perhaps the boys might show her attention, though that could lead to jealousy from the indigenous female school population.

Right, Morrissey, block it out. Hurry up, you depressing git; she said to herself as she dropped her chin beneath her thick woollen scarf to counter the cold October breeze.

'I was happy in the haze of a drunken hour but heaven knows I'm miserable nowww.'

Yeah, that's right, she sighed.

The timetable was already ingrained in her memory: PE first period. There's nothing like integrating yourself with new classmates by cutting about in ill-fitting, red nylon shorts and a decrepit white top.

She cringed in anticipation.

This was where she found herself, walking the tarmac footpath adjacent to a waterlogged, rutted, football pitch, its rusted uprights reflected in the deep puddles that surrounded them, to a building that seemed more forbidding with every step.

'Right, girls, pay attention,' roared the track-suited female teacher. 'Get changed quickly and into the big hall for netball in five minutes. Oh, and we have a new member of our happy team.' She hurriedly read the registration sheet. 'Where's Mairi ... err ... Mairi-Clare Smyth. Where are you Mairi-Clare?' she called, scanning the room for an unfamiliar face.

'Miss,' she announced timidly, raising her hand awkwardly in the air.

'Welcome Mairi-Clare, I'm Mrs Gray. Pleased to meet you. These girls will look after you.' She smirked, pointing around the room, her eyes fixed on the new classmate. 'Stay away from the Saint Saviour boys, not worth the effort,' she advised, which was greeted by a cheer. She processed her new pupil's flawless features, high cheekbones and piercing blue eyes, which complemented her curled fair hair. 'Now, it's two minutes, girls.'

'Don't listen to her. We've got a few cute boys worth getting bothered about. I'm Tricia. Hurry up 'n' get changed. She'll be back in bawling again in a minute,' a nearby schoolmate advised.

Mairi-Clare followed the girl's lead, removing her tie and blouse, putting on her white T-shirt then reaching for her skirt.

'I'm not looking, girls. I'm not looking!'

Mairi-Clare was startled as screams and horrified yells erupted around her.

'Get out, ya perv...'

'Weirdo...'

'Sir, yer not allowed in here!'

Half-dressed, Mairi-Clare stood rigid, her blouse covering her bare legs and exposed pants. A man stood inside the changing-room door. His hand covered his eyes, though he seemed to be peering through his fingers. His face was heavily wrinkled and his short grey hair accompanied a faded blue tracksuit.

'I'm not looking, girls. Just to inform you of a change of plan. You are in the wee gym hall today.'

'Aye, right, ya mad pervert. Get out!' screamed one red-faced girl.

The teacher made his exit to a crescendo of hisses and catcalls.

'That's the boys PE teacher. Pops in from time to time to try 'n' get a swatch of us undressed. We just give him pelters.'

'I feel sorry for the first years,' sniggered a class member.

'If you've a wee sister in first year, warn her. Come tae think of it, if you have a wee brother warn him tae. He looks down the boys' shorts to scan for pant wearers. He's just eyeing up their arses.'

'I don't know what to say,' Mairi-Clare whispered in reply as she quickly finished dressing.

'You'll get used to it. Come on, missus, time for pishy netball,' Tricia remarked, clutching her newfound friend's arm.

Mairi-Clare's day was becoming draining.

'We have a new pupil,' announced Mrs William, the over-exuberant, hefty music teacher from the back of the class. Mairi-Clare shrank in her chair. *Roll on next week*, she thought, *when I'm nobody again*.

'And one whom, I may say, is an accomplished violinist and guitarist. A talent which I hope will rub off on you lot while you screech through the recorder,' she sneered, dipping the well-worn plastic instruments in disinfectant and distributing them to the underwhelmed pupils in preparation for the forthcoming lesson.

For the last three and a half years, Mairi-Clare had been accustomed to the best of everything at fee-paying St Mark's. Provided with the latest materials and textbooks, as well as the continued challenge and expectation placed on pupils to achieve top marks, it was hard not to thrive.

All that had changed quite dramatically with the closure of the profitable Talbot car plant in Linwood and the loss of 13,000 jobs. Despite producing the Sunbeam, the best-selling small car in Britain, of which her father had sold thousands of units, the factory had fallen foul of a new type of Britain in which neither Linwood's nor his skills were required.

Her father had taken it particularly badly. Being head of sales for the UK brought its benefits, and no expense was spared to ensure all the family enjoyed an extravagant lifestyle. That had vanished quickly. Her parents, John and Clare Smyth, were now hawking themselves around companies across Britain, desperately looking for employment of a similar stature that would allow them to recapture the lifestyle to which they were accustomed – and one that was fast becoming a distant memory.

Two major changes had occurred: the luxury villa and stables they called home in Kilmacolm was repossessed just three months after the first default on the mortgage payments, and the private schooling was sacrificed for the less salubrious surroundings of Saviour High. Less than two years after the factory gates closed, the redundancy pot was empty and their lives had changed forever.

Clare Smyth, or McGettigan as she was prior to marriage, had been born and raised in Paisley's West End with her four siblings. Her parents, now long gone, had earned a living by cleaning the houses of rich people and working on building sites. This was where she returned with John and the two children, to the old family home in Walkin St in the heart of the West End.

'Good view of the bowling green,' John quipped, as the family peered out of the bay window of the second-floor Victorian flat. 'We'd better enjoy watching it because we've got hee-haw money to do anything else.'

* * *

Mikey gazed at the new class member, the plastic recorder wedged in the side of his mouth.

'Put yer eyes back in, Mikey boy. You've no chance with her,' Tubbs sniggered.

'She's gorgeous. She's the one, Tubsy boy,' he replied, his eyes fixed on his latest challenge.

'Aye, right. Thought that Sarah Watts was *the one,* that no' just last week?' Tubbs retorted, nudging his mate in the ribs. Mikey maintained his fixed gape.

'Michael Mulheron, that recorder is not a lollipop,' barked Mrs William, her body vibrating with every syllable. 'Put it back in the cleanser and accompany your new classmate to the school office with these registration papers. I don't want Mairi-Clare getting lost in this warren of a building.'

Tubbs sniggered. Mikey froze. He walked briskly to the rear of the class and deposited the recorder in the basin while taking the opportunity to run his hands through his hair, tuck in his shirt and tighten his stomach muscles before he strode confidently towards the class door.

She looked stunning, he thought, as Mairi-Clare stood up, her curls dancing softly above her small shoulders, her gaze catching his hazel eyes as he held the door open. He would have to think quickly on his feet, he thought, to secure a date as no doubt there would be competition from other suitors for her attention in the weeks ahead.

'I'm Michael.'

'I heard,' she retorted dismissively, pausing beside the closed classroom door. He stopped in the unoccupied corridor and stared like a docile puppy awaiting his master's instructions.

'Well ... which way?' she asked impatiently.

'Oh, sorry, follow me,' he replied nervously, slowly heading down the colourless hallway.

'So yer into yer music then?' he asked, breaking the silence.

'Apparently.'

'Me 'n' Tubbs love it too. Not that shite auld William does but a huge variety of stuff.'

'Such as?'

'Err, och, loads. Ye know, wide range,' he stuttered. 'Classical opera-type stuff, rock, and new romantic, mod – anything at all. We're starting a band. We've still tae decide whit music style tae adopt 'n' that. Yer more than welcome to join if yer as good as she says.' He flicked his head back towards the music department.

'I just might do that, Mister Mike,' she replied, catching and holding his stare, causing him to fail to navigate the fire extinguisher hanging on the wall.

'Ya dirty bastard!' he screamed, rubbing his injured knee. 'Sorry, not you, that thing.'

Her eyes danced with laughter. *This is too easy*, she thought.

'We're meeting round at Tubbs house on Friday to come up with a plan. That's the lovable fat guy sitting next to me. If ye want to join us, I could meet ye beforehand. Up to you, doesn't matter if ye don't but be good if ye could, though.'

'Okay, I'll come.'

'If yer not allowed, or it's not yer thing, it doesn't...'

'I'll come, daft boy! Now shut up and take me to the office.'

Chapter Four

'HI, DAD, THAT'S ME IN.'

'The Prime Minister welcomed the United States President, Ronald Reagan, and wife Nancy to Number 10 Downing Street, further endorsing the special relationship between not only the world's most powerful countries but the two most influential and prominent leaders on the planet.' The TV blared, projecting the mid-afternoon news.

'Maggie Thatcher? Maggie Thatcher?' Peter screamed at the Radio Rental twenty-inch screen in the corner of the living room, his face contorted with disgust, forcing veins to expand along his neckline as if in preparation for battle.

'*FUCK HER.*' He raised two fingers aggressively at the image of the British political leader on the screen. '*FUCK HER.*'

'*DAD*,' screamed Lizzy, grabbing her father's attention, causing him to face her with a startle.

'Sorry, Elizabeth. Sorry, love. How was yer day?'

'Turn that down, Dad. Have you been sitting there all day?' she asked incredulously, pointing at the well-worn, floral-embossed armchair.

'No darling, not at all,' he replied, moving to greet his only daughter. 'Ah've been down the Bru. Waste of time right enough but always good to keep your self-esteem levels in check.' His trip to the Job Centre was similar to countless others over the past three years.

A qualified millwright, Peter had worked for more than twenty-five years with a small family business. A thriving, growing concern and the main contractor to Paisley's two thread mills, all was going well. The company had earned a profitable living customising layouts and installing new machinery within the huge facilities churning out thread, which was distributed worldwide. He loved his job and the company that employed him, George Winters & Co. The proprietor was a quiet, unassuming man with an entrepreneur's eye for business and opportunity.

Mr Winters was on the lookout for fresh, more lucrative contracts further afield than the company's traditional Paisley base. The news filled Peter and his fellow employees with great confidence for their long-term prospects, and led Peter to accumulate what savings he had and approach his boss with a proposal.

'Peter, son, I could take your money, no problem and to be honest it would come in right handy. I say that without hesitation, recourse or favour. That I would be proud to have you, a great family man and leader, as a business partner is unquestionable. However, it would be dishonest. You know I keep a keen eye on the business world. The shift in the Teutonic plates is astonishing, Peter.' Mr Winters walked his employee from the deafening machine assembly-room floor, with grinders cutting metal and forges aflame heating and softening iron so it could be shaped by heavy hammers and brute strength, to the compact office he occupied at least six days a week.

What a great orator you'd make, Mr Winters, Peter thought, *but friggin' get on with it.*

'I'm looking for new contracts, that is correct. Not to *expand* the business but to keep us from going under, son,' Mr Winters announced dejectedly, brushing his grey, Brylcreemed hair back into place while glancing at his employee's large, imposing frame to gauge his reaction.

Peter raised his thick eyebrows then laughed. 'You're shitting me, right?'

'No, sorry I'm not,' Mr Winters replied.

'But we're snowed under!' Peter exclaimed, trying to process this new information. 'I've worked the last eight weekends, sixty-hour weeks, Mr Winters, and the work is flying in. Christ, even that, lazy tosser Kerr has stepped it up to help us out!'

'I know son. But it's short-term gain. Make the most of it while I can offer it,' the owner replied, patting his wallet. 'Look, Peter, I've been in this game thirty-five years servicing those mills. I've made a handsome living out of it, as they have me. The game changer was Mrs Thatcher winning in 1979. Industry is finished; they've removed the need of the country to rely on manufacturing. Dismantled that powerbase, that sense of community created by generations, and placed the emphasis on getting rich around her southern electoral headquarters. Those in privileged positions can do so and all the others can sink or swim,' he exclaimed, raising his arms in frustration.

'What the hell is that to do wae' us? The work's piling in, man!' Peter was beginning to express frustration with his employer. Mr Winter liked nothing better than to exhibit his wide vocabulary and knowledge to his employees who, although he respected them, he did not consider to be his equal.

'Peter, without a doubt the mills will be given notice to shut in around eighteen months. Don't ask how I know but it will – and I repeat – *will* happen. We are a supplier in the food chain. The work will be delivered cheaper abroad and this right-wing government won't fight to keep it here.' He sighed, slumping in the chair, while raising invoices from his untidy desk and throwing them on the office floor.

'This means, we'll go beforehand,' he added quietly. 'You're an intelligent man. You know there's no way they'll order from us once the word is out. That's why I seek out new contracts, but to no avail. I surmise we have eight months, maybe a year at best. Sorry.' He placed his head in his hands, his red, broken skin peering through his thick stump-like fingers.

'I'm sorry, Mr Winters. I know how much this outfit means to you. I'm fucking shocked, 'scuse the cursing.' Peter sighed and slumped downhearted in the corner of the office. He had envisaged seeing out his days here and welcoming his son, Michael, into the business in three years' time once he was of age to leave school to carry on a working legacy.

Michael, not academically minded, was already counting the days until he could say goodbye to Saviours High and get a job, have some money in his pocket and indulge in his real loves – music, football and girls.

Three years on, and with 1984 entering autumn, Peter's redundancy cheque had long disappeared and it seemed hard to recall the life they'd had previously. It hadn't been extravagant but it had been comfortable, with Christmas always taken care of, food on the table, a couple of pound guaranteed each week for some beer and the annual much-anticipated holiday back in County Donegal, the place they all considered home. All of that was long gone, a distant memory. Life had become a daily struggle to get by, surviving on Ellen's dinner-lady wages and his fortnightly giro.

The hopelessness of it all frustrated him. Forty-five years old, and he was being told by snotty Jobcentre staff that his working days and any meaningful contribution he could make had ceased when he was handed his P45 by an inconsolable Mr Winters. The government of the day decided that a winner-takes-all mentality and individualism were the preferred methods of a successful nation.

Now both parties were playing out the charade: him desperately seeking work, and the Jobcentre accepting his efforts as a justification for posting out his meagre allowance.

Mr Winters lasted three weeks into his forced retirement before a massive heart attack claimed him. Another victim of Thatcher's Britain.

'This is Sarah, Dad,' announced Lizzy, stepping aside to reveal her friend. She put an arm around her friend's nervous, now scared, diminutive frame.

'Nice to meet you, Sarah, and welcome to our humble abode,' Peter said with a snigger and a wistful look around the living room.

'And you, Mr Mulheron.'

'Please, call me Peter. Sorry about that. Please don't be frightened,' he added, sensing her fear. 'That wummin just gets me riled.'

Sarah looked down self-consciously and then towards Lizzy for guidance. Lizzy smiled and rubbed her friend's arm to reassure her.

'Dad, Sarah goes to Martin Special School, the one across from ours. We're doing a joint project with St Mary's Church – should be fun,' Lizzy said, depositing their school bags on the floor and heading into the narrow, scullery kitchen.

'Gutted. That new girl I was telling you about, Dad? Mairi-Thingummy? She got a singing part just because she can strum a guitar – badly – and play the violin. Ha!' Lizzy's voice projected throughout the ground-floor tenement flat, echoing off the high Victorian walls and ornate ceilings.

Peter glanced at Sarah; he made cat claws and contorted his face, forcing his young visitor to laugh. 'Oh, what a shame you didn't get *that* part.' He raised his voice in reply, while sinking his mouth under his faded T-shirt.

'Not bothered, Dad,' Lizzy replied, striding into the room, 'Sarah and me are doin' bidding prayers. We need to come up with them ourselves. No probs, eh, Sarah?'

'Yes, really looking forward to it,' her new friend replied timidly.

'That's why we're here. We got three weeks to get it ready – it's homework. Oh sorry, more homework.'

'Well, I'll leave you to it,' Peter said. 'I'll call in on Dixie and see if he's any spare work going. Sarah, nice meeting you and I look forward to see you round here more often and at St Mary's. That's where Elizabeth and Michael were christened. Wouldn't fit in the font now.' He grinned and winked, then turned to his daughter. 'Bye, love. I'll be back in an hour to make the tea. Not be much, I'm afraid. Lecky needs paid and the giro isn't here till Monday.' His animation drained as he switched on again to his family's never-ending predicament.

Lizzy sensed his torment, as did her visitor. 'No probs, Dad,' she said, grabbing his waist and squeezing tightly. 'Whatever we have, you'll burn it.' She giggled to ease the tension.

'She is funny, Sarah, eh? Talking of Michael, where's he at?' Peter asked, slipping his worn combat jacket over his broad shoulders and stooping to place a kiss on his daughter's head.

'Mikey's round at Tubbs' house, said he'll be in for tea. Starting a band up, he says. Ha, what a laugh that'll be! More to do with Mairi-Thingummy, I imagine. Bye, Dad, love you. Is Mum back tonight?' Lizzy shouted, slanting her head to hear his reply.

'Aw right. Naw, love, yer grandpa's no' great. Be tomorrow. Don't worry, you'll survive ma cooking a couple of days yet.' He pulled the front door shut behind him.

'Right Sarah,' Lizzy said. 'Custard creams, tea and bidding prayers.'

Chapter Five

'**G**OOD MORNING. YOU MUST be Mr Lynch. You are very welcome.'

'And you must be Ms Knox,' Cal replied, smiling broadly as he walked towards the middle-aged woman dressed in a two-piece, silver-grey suit and frilly blouse. *Most likely from Goldbergs*, he thought. 'It's great to be here at last.'

'May I first of all apologise for yesterday, Mr Lynch. We assumed you would be taking over the business from today. It was a tiresome day and we try to vacate the office for some respite at lunchtime to allow us to remain focused in the afternoon,' she said hesitantly. She left the confines of her desk and met him in the middle of the office. 'May I also complement you on your attire? Hand-made in Savile Row, if I'm not mistaken? Herringbone tweed.' She observed the sharp cut of his suit, complemented with a light-blue button-down shirt, gold tie and matching cufflinks and tiepin. 'I've a very keen eye when it comes to quality material.'

She clearly had an acute sense of admitting misdemeanours while enshrouding them in compliments. *Once I get her loyalty*, he thought, *she'll be a great asset*. 'No problem, Ms Knox. Or shall I call you Anne?'

'Why, of course you can.' She observed his distinctive brown eyes that continually scanned the sparse office, taking everything in.

'Please call me Cal.'

'I prefer formalities, especially around clients, Mr Lynch.'

'Of course, quite correct.' She was laying down a marker; first point to her. Let her have it – he was the boss after all.

'Our colleague, Mr Joyce, is delivering papers to the procurator fiscal's office at present. He shouldn't be too long. I hope you don't mind but I've begun allocating time in your diary for this week, though I have left this morning free for you to settle in. Your first appointment is with a potential client at 2pm. I thought you would like the office vacated by your predecessor. It is the more spacious of the two, and has a big window with clear views onto the Wellmeadow. As well as having less dampness on the walls,' she added, gesturing at the black patches and woodchip wallpaper lifting off the walls.

'Excellent, Ms Knox. I've just got a few boxes to bring in.' He moved towards the door.

'Sorry, we assume you will want to make changes to the business. Staff, maybe?' she called after him, slightly lowering her voice.

'Nothing that can't wait or will kill us, Ms Knox. Don't worry.'

Cal quickly made himself at home. He rearranged the desk to view the front door of the main office, which looked on to West Brae and the busy thoroughfare of Wellmeadow Street. His primary objective was to observe the comings, goings and, more importantly, the dynamics of his new business rather than taking in the delights of the grey urban scenery and its population.

The space under the window was an ideal position for his record player and the boxes of LPs which accompanied him wherever he worked.

He settled back in the dusty leather chair; it creaked with every movement. He thought about how far he had come in the past twenty-two years and time seemed to shrink in those few short moments. The thoughts and feelings that were the driving force behind his relentless motivation never left him. His eyes closed momentarily as memories of his father returned; he saw him rubbing his strong fingers over his skull as Cal sat at his feet playing with his cars and building tunnels with the thick fireplace rug. He could feel the sense of warmth and security that he had failed to emulate since.

This wasn't revenge; it wasn't about getting even but about putting right a wrong. *He ruined my life. Now I'll demolish his.*

'Ms Knox, my office with Mr Joyce as soon as he's back, okay?' he called via the internal line.

'Very good, Mr Lynch. He shouldn't be too far away.'

The door slammed and he heard a muffled conversation in the front office. With a light tap, his new secretary entered accompanied by her colleague. 'Mr Joyce has returned, Mr Lynch,' she said.

Rising to his feet, he met his new employee at the front of the dark-oak desk. No need to be too formal yet. 'Pleased to meet you Mr Joyce.'

The man stood around five feet eight, had a dishevelled appearance and seemed to be sweating profusely. His thinning black hair was swept from left to right, fighting against an emerging bald spot.

'And you, Mr Lynch. Please call me Jack or Jackie. Bit out of breath here. Had to make the PF's first thing with witness papers for a defendant. Guilty as sin, the wee thug, but we are here to represent, aren't we?'

'Indeed, Jack,' Cal replied, his mind racing to the next part of the planned conversation. 'Take a seat, please.' He perched between them on the edge of the desk. 'I just want to run through a couple of points. First thing, there will be no payoffs or new staff coming in. It's the three of us for the foreseeable future.' He scanned their eyes and body language. All good so far.

'Secondly, I've obviously read through the caseloads, the accounts and, more importantly, each of your roles in keeping this place functioning when things got, shall we say, tough. Thank you for doing that. I may implement changes in the coming months and I am really looking forward to growing the business,' he added, walking round his desk, thankfully recalling his squeaky chair before sitting down. It would have ruined his impact. 'But we'll do it as a team – or, if we can't agree, I'll decide,' he advised them assertively.

Jack had encountered five new owners in the twelve years he'd worked in the West End. Each one was either burned out by a monotonous, enormous caseload or sold up to move onto bigger, better things. One incumbent, Gordon McIntosh, saddled with gambling debt and a growing dependency on cocaine, had succumbed to gangster pressure that resulted in him being struck off and receiving a custodial for smuggling drugs to clients on remand in HMP Barlinnie. McIntosh had arrived at the law practice with the same enthusiasm the new incumbent was currently displaying, he thought. That all changed a mere ten months of his tenure when new client files were created which only the lawyer himself had access to. His demeanour became increasingly detached and the day to day business of low level criminal cases was continually ignored. Upon his arrest, the office was turned over by local police officers and the secret files were removed shortly before a full-scale raid by plain clothed officers from Glasgow, accompanied by inland revenue colleagues arrived with a warrant to seize all documents. McIntosh was in deep and knew more than he should have. He refused to co-operate or answer questions during days of interrogation. He knew his fate and accepted he would be jailed, his promising career over. Keeping his mouth shut would ensure he would be well looked after once he arrived at the prison to see out his sentence.

'Sounds fine to me, boss,' responded Jack, glancing over his shoulder towards the uninterrupted, blue sky that was struggling to break through the dirt-encased window and bring some brightness to the dimly lit room

'So, it's business as usual. I'll arrange a weekly team meeting with Ms Knox. That's all for now.' Cal's eyes unintentionally steered them both towards the door. 'Ms Knox, just a couple of things. Get our landlord on the phone about the damp, please. I'm not paying rent for a dump. And forward our new details to all the local police stations for the relevant desk sergeants. Can you get hold of a joiner, preferably local? I want a clear glass door on here and we need a new sign out front. Make sure I am here when this work is carried out. And also organise a weekly window clean, inside and out. Oh, and the signage. The wording is, "Cal Lynch, Criminal Defence Lawyers". Thank you.' He thought that sounded fantastic.

'I'll deal with that straight away and have drafts and quotes by close today. Once I contact Mill Street Police Station, you'll be added to the on-call rota, Mr Lynch,' Ms Knox replied, pulling the door closed behind her. Then she put her head round it again. 'Oh, and Mr Lynch.' A mixture of laughter lines and wrinkles appeared on her face. 'Welcome to Paisley.'

Chapter Six

'WHAT THE HELL'S GOING on in there, Gracie? Some racket!' Dixie made his way across the cluttered room, shuffling to avoid washing baskets and the well-worn trappings of a busy kitchen.

He had never fully acclimatised to the household chaos that a family inevitably created, and he was constantly agitated when he came home from a shift. Three young boys, all diverse and special in their own way, kept him and his high-school sweetheart, Grace Docherty, on their toes.

He looked over his shoulder still searching for an answer as he scrubbed the oil from his hands with the pink carbolic soap.

'Dixie, leave them be,' his wife responded. Her voice rose, emphasising her stress as she transferred the wet clothes to the spin compartment of the twin-tub washer. 'Terence is setting things up. Fur the first time, Joe is interested in something other than an excuse fur no gaun tae school,'

Grace's days were erratically busy. Keeping the house ticking over while working as a part-time cleaner in the evenings and ensuring her

three boys did not stray too far off the straight and narrow fully occupied each waking minute.

The oldest of five siblings, her strained looks belied her age. Her
tough upbringing in Ferguslie Park included a mother who died in
childbirth and a father who spent any money he earned on drink in the
New Fergus Hotel at the eastern edge of a sprawling estate known
lovingly as 'The Scheme'.

She was suitably proud of her achievements. From the age of fourteen, she had ensured her three sisters and brother were clean, fed and
never missed school. They were all now making their way successfully
in the world.

Grace clutched at any glimmer of hope that would ease her worry
and allow her mind to rest. She was exhausted with the constant battle
to enthuse and motivate her children to realise their potential. Joe, her
thirteen-year-old son, was continuously breaking her heart. She was on
first-name terms with the school's truant officer; she feared the day she'd
have to stand in front of the sheriff and receive a custodial sentence due
to Joe's habitual lack of attendance. Stephen, her youngest, was so full of
energy there were repeated visits to his guidance teacher. The next stop
for him would be Doctor McMillan; Valium for her good self and something to slow young Stephen down would make life easier.

At fifteen and a half, Terence was the oldest and he provided the
most contentment. She disliked the Tubbs' nickname he was labelled
with, mainly because it made her feel guilty about his weight, which in
part was her fault. Terence hated physical education after being humil-
iated in his first year of high school. At a swimming lesson, an aggressive supply teacher sent Terence to the deep end of the pool, dismissing
his protests. The teacher guessed that, as he was wearing trunks with
four swimming badges sewn onto them, he must be an accomplished
swimmer. Unfortunately the trunks belonged to a neighbour because
Grace couldn't afford to buy new ones. Terence had to be rescued from
the bottom of the pool by a lifeguard and never ventured near PE again.

These constant worries, coupled with Dixie's wayward, adolescent outlook on life, ensured time had passed quickly together with her engaging youthful looks.

'Just asking, love. Sounds like the Barralands in there,' replied Dixie, drying his hands on his faded T-shirt.

'Och, wheesht, will ye!' she snapped. 'You make more noise when ye come in pished at the weekend.'

Her eyes locked with her husband's as she worked her way through a mountain of dry washing, separating, folding and stacking. 'Look, Terence and Michael are putting together some band. Joe and his wee pal want tae join, so let them be for today, will ye?' she lamented. 'This town's going to rack 'n ruin wae junkies and scumbags peddling hash or smack to anyone weak enough to fall into their trap. If a band keeps any of them from being tempted tae fall into their dirty clutches, yer bloody ears will need tae be sacrificed.'

'Awright! Whoa.' Dixie moved to give her a reassuring hug. 'No probs, darling. A band? Ah kin sing like fuck.' He laughed, about to burst into song.

Grace stopped him in his tracks, nipping his lips with her fingers. 'Aye, right. Don't think they'll be playing any Val Doonican, ya idiot,' she replied, throwing a clean towel at his face. 'Use that next time, ya clat!'

* * *

Mikey paced nervously. He prayed she'd show, though he was far from convinced she would.

He'd spent the early evening preparing for the meet and choosing what to wear to make an impression. He'd finally selected his grey Sta-Press trousers, white polo shirt and red Harrington, his favourite piece of clothing. He was particular about his appearance but limited their use – these were his best clothes and there was no sign of replacements coming any time soon.

He'd bought them with his first provident cheque that he'd received for his last birthday. He felt he was finally grown up when he took the cheque to the town to buy his own gear. The provi man had changed; his dad's mate Eddie Toner had done it for years, and wasn't too fussed when repayments were missed now and again. Eddie had packed it in due to a spate of muggings. Owing to the increased frequency the new provi man came to the house looking for his weekly return, coupled with the excessive interest rates and his dad ignoring the continuous ringing of the doorbell, Mikey assumed that the new relationship was not as flexible. New gear was not on the horizon any time soon.

Setting up a band was sharp thinking. Showing an interest in her hobbies would go in his favour. He had strategically chosen the Big Apple as the meeting point. The large, popular amusement arcade situated on Broomland Street in the bustling West End had previously been a cinema. Now it attracted youths from all over the town. Mikey's thinking was that if any of his pals clocked him standing outside getting a potential dizzy, he would have the excuse of waiting on Tubbs to play pool.

He began to daydream as the sun warmed him. Leaning against the white, roughcast, wall, he looked down Queen Street to his old primary school playground. *Happy days in St Mary's*, he thought. *Eat your lunch, run across the road, past Tannahill the Poet's cottage, up to the playground for a sidey – same teams from the game that kicked off before 9am until last playtime.*

'Hello, Mr Mike.'

Her voice startled him, shaking him from his daydream. 'Hiya. Ye turned up.'

'You sound surprised,' she responded.

'You look great.'

She looked down: baby Doc boots, Levi's and black check shirt. Hardly vogue. 'So where's this *event* taking place?' she enquired.

'Tubbs' hoose stays doon here in Argyle Street, two minutes' walk,' he replied, pointing eastwards and leading her down the small slope of Queen Street.

A rich caustic odour of heated metal still hung in the air, its heaviness catching their throats as they turned left onto Cross Street where the small industrial units sat adjacent to the playground of his old school now redundant of the youthful weekday noise. Their destination, the large tenement properties, came into view and dominated the skyline. The structures were a small, eternal symbol of the town's rich industrial past.

Mikey remained nervous as they walked in silence. He was seldom tongue-tied around girls. His telegenic looks, infectious personality and smooth tongue usually gave him the edge over his peers. But Mairi-Clare unsettled him with her confidence and attitude – maybe that was the challenge. She seemed totally in control and Mikey struggled as to how he could influence her feelings towards him. He decided only to speak when he thought he had something positive, interesting or meaningful to say that would impress her. They continued in silence.

'Err, this is Tubbs' close,' he finally announced. 'Used tae run businesses from the hooses back in the day. Ye can still see the names oan the side of the close,' he added, pointing to the weathered sandstone entrance and leading the way up the dimly lit steps. The natural light on the landing was transformed into colourful beams of red, blues and greens by the large, stained-glass, windows.

'Yep, my gran ran a dressmaker's in Walkin Street for thirty years. So my mum says. That's where I stay. If you weren't so secretive, you could have saved us both a walk.' Her voice echoed throughout the wide stairwells as she teasingly pushed him down the well-worn steps.

'Mikey, come in.' Grace greeted them with a smile, the heat emanating from the flat warming their skin. 'Whose yer wee pal?' she queried, guiding them into the hallway.

'Mairi-Clare, Mrs Clark. No' long moved intae the West End,' he replied.

'Welcome and God help ye hen ... only kidding. Right, listen. Joe and his pal – whit's his name?' she asked, glancing quickly at Mikey.

'Shada.'

'His real name!' she scolded.

'Err, Shadow?' He shrugged.

'Anyway, they want to try out for your band. Do not slag them, encourage them,' Grace hissed in a low voice. 'I've not seen our Joe so enthusiastic since the Co-op introduced pound slots in the shopping trolleys.'

'No probs, Mrs Clark. Is Tub ... sorry, Terence in?'

'Aye, just go into the living room. He has it all set up.'

'Awrite, mate.'

'Aye, Tubbs. You?'

'Welcome to Chateau Clark, Mairi-Clare. Or should that be Shit-hole Clark,' Tubbs announced, guiding his guest to a single, stained, cream-leather seat.

'What the fuck ... sorry,' exclaimed Mikey, catching a glimpse of a shiny, ruby-red drumkit taking pride of place in the spacious living room.

'Lovely drumkit, Terence,' Mairi-Clare said, spinning the sticks in her hand.

'Call me Tubbs.'

'I prefer Terence. More distinct, if I'm honest. But if you insist,' Mairi-Clare responded assertively.

'It's Joe's, Mikey. Don't know where the hell he got it. Boy's a rocket. He's away tae get Shada.'

'May as well wait for them then? Yer maw gave us gip on the way in, so don't be giving the wee man a hard time, all right? Everyone got their choices?' he asked, exerting control and eyeballing his friends.

They didn't have to wait long. The silence was broken by two dapper, red-faced teenagers who had clearly struggled with the rush up the stairs as they burst through the mahogany-stained door.

'Sorry for the haud up, troops. Had tae pick up this stand,' announced Joe, placing the mic in front of the drumkit, which was nestling beside three large bay windows.

'Joe, where the hell did ye get this gear?' his brother queried in a whisper.

'George fae the Record Market owes me 'n' Shada a turn. We've been sticking posters up around the toon the last three weeks, some band playing in the Toon Hall. He's punting the tickets. This gear's the support band's. Ah need tae get it back the night... The clobber?' he added, tugging on his Fred Perry button-down shirt and looking towards his dogtooth Sta-Press, 'is fae our money-making ventures. No' bad, eh?' he smirked, looking round the room expectantly.

'Ye look great, wee man. Right, let's get this gaun. Who's first?' Mikey asked, moving to the centre of the room with an air of urgency.

'Me 'n' Shada, troops. This gear's tae be back soon.'

'And yer suggestion?' asked his exasperated brother.

'Look, we need something to make us cash, right? Well, this mob will help dae jist that. They're loaded. Tubbs, The Jam, side two, track one,' he replied, pointing towards the smoked-glass Panasonic record player and stack of vinyl LPs sitting on top of the ornate pine dresser.

Tubbs removed the glossy black vinyl from the sleeve. The edginess of the cover, with band members pictured in front of self-prophesised graffiti, set the scene for the forthcoming tune.

'Ah'm miming, obviously, but listen tae Shada. *He's* playing these bad boys, amazing he is. Make sure it's nice 'n' loud, Tubbs.' He wrapped his hands around the mic, lowered his head, and fixed his eyes on his two-tone bowling shoes, awaiting his cue.

A crescendo of bass guitar filled the room, followed by Shada springing to life with precision drumming. The music brought the room and its inhabitants to life. Joe worked the mic and his lip-synching was impeccable. The boy manipulating the drumkit seemed to have come out of nowhere and produced a faultless delivery that was far removed from the quiet, unassuming personality who was constantly in Joe's shade.

The two had been inseparable since the first day of Primary One at St Mary's. Joe had been inconsolable at having to leave his mother to enter the imposing black, iron, school gates. He thought she'd never come back. Shada had shared his packed lunch and made him laugh, which distracted Joe from his worries.

Their lives were now intertwined, always looking for money-making opportunities and sharing takings equally. Many thought Joe dominated his diminutive friend, though the pals knew differently; Shada was the brains. His more outgoing partner was the frontman.

Dixie swung his wife around the kitchen, her red hair flowing loosely over her shoulders, as the music blared from across the hall. 'Yer no' a bad mover, Gracie. Takes me back tae when Ah used tae nip ye up the dancing.'

'Ah had many a name oan ma card, Dix. Consider yourself lucky,' she laughed.

'Bloody hell, ye kin hear that racket doon the street.' Peter entered the kitchen laughing at his childhood friends' antics. 'Ah found this yin outside,' he added, grasping the shoulders of the youngest Clark brood.

'Join in, Big Man, music's brilliant.'

'Dad, kin a get a month's pocket money, please?' the small boy asked in a soft voice, slumping on a chair and staring sadly at the floor.

'Whit?' replied Dixie, concentrating on maintaining the beat with his dance partner.

'Ah need tae buy lino!'

'Stephen, whit you oan aboot?'

'This stuff, lino!' Stephen replied, stamping the square-patterned cream floor to emphasise his point. 'Ah'm part of a break-dancing crew – Managers of Mayhem. Blazer bought the ghetto blaster, Frame got the trackies 'n' Ah've got tae get the lino! We're against the Bronx soon,' he whinged, his face contorted with stress that belied his years.

'Gracie, ah cannae keep up wae' these weans,' Dixie laughed.

'Stephen, we will sort it,' his mother reassured him, running her fingers through his unkempt shoulder-length hair.

'Better! Or am oot a' the Crew 'n' ma name's Shuffle,' he scolded, making his way towards the kitchen door. The adults stifled their laughter to save the boy's feelings.

'And how kin we no huv Alpine?' he shouted, slamming the door behind him.

'Shuffle? Boys no' half wise,' quipped Dixie, 'He wanted tae be Boy George last week.'

'Even worse, he wants tae drink that shitty Alpine,' laughed Peter.

33

Shada lowered the drumsticks while Joe surveyed the reaction to their performance around the room.

Mairi-Clare broke the silence. 'I really enjoyed that. It was very upbeat, energetic, with a fair amount of passion. Very well done, you two. Shadow, where did you learn to play like that?' She tilted her head to catch the younger boy's eye.

Shada shrugged. 'My Da used tae have an auld kit in the shed.'

Mikey was worried. How would his conquest view his proposal? 'Great boys, don't think we need to make a decision until we have heard all the suggestions, awright?'

'Right, nae bother. Let us know,' Joe responded, wiping the sweat from his brow with his sleeve, while beginning a mini de-rig of the borrowed equipment. 'Me 'n' Shada need tae get the kit back up the road. Keep George happy.'

The removal led to a vacant space around the bay windows, which Mikey chose to occupy.

'Kin we call ye Mairi ... or MC?' Tubbs interjected, stretching his body out on the comfortable sofa.

'Is Mairi-Clare too much like hard work?' She smiled. 'Of course you can, I'm not precious.' She ruffled her hair and held Tubbs' glance.

'Right, who's next,' Mikey interjected, feeling slightly left out and recognising something may be growing between his latest conquest and his best pal.

Tubbs rose slowly from the couch. 'Right, be prepared to be mesmerised, enthralled and inspired all at the wan time. I'm gonnae play something which will blow ye away and awaken your inner spirit.' He paused, eyeballing his audience. 'But enough of me. Sit back, close your eyes and slip into the mesmerising glow of...'

He anxiously moved the needle over the spinning vinyl, carefully finding the correct track. 'This is an auld album Ah got fae the Record Market's discount bin but they sound brilliant. A group fae Africa. The guy that runs them is called Joseph Shabalala. Whit a name, eh? This is *Awu Wemmmadoda* by Ladysmith Black err ... Ladysmith Black Mombazo!'

The haunting capella sound of bass, alto and tenor male voices shrouded the room. The mesmerising tones caused sudden goosebumps on Mairi-Clare's skin as she became engrossed in the harmony. Mikey closed his eyes to allow his mind to concentrate fully on the evocative sounds.

'Whit the hell they listening tae noo?' Dixie sniggered.

'God knows. You any work going, mate?' Peter enquired. 'Need tae get oot the hoose. Even just a couple of hours tae help ye oot?'

'Am no huving ye help me without paying. Ah've nothing just noo, but got a couple a' prices in. I'll let ye know.' Whispering, he added, 'Might be heading for the jail for whit a done tae that auld Fitzgerald's front door the other week. Gaun tae that new lawyer oan Monday.'

'Feck sake, hope not, Dix. Serves ye right though, ya nutter,' Peter laughed. 'Ah might go oan the taxis just for a wee while, though the thought a' working for that scumbag Quinn turns ma stomach.'

Dixie shook his head emphatically. 'Things must be right shite if you'd dae that.'

'Aye, they are. It's no great.' Peter sighed, staring numbly out onto the manicured back garden. The well-laid out plots signified resident territory, with an assortment of huts and vegetable patches colliding with each other and, from his view on the third floor, merging into the earth's surface.

Tubbs removed the needle arm from the vinyl, content with his submission.

'I like it, Terence. Very emotional,' said Mairi-Clare.

'Tubbs, very good, mate. But just a couple of things: one we're no black, and two we cannae sing African,' interjected Mikey, shaking his head.

'Zulu.'

'Eh?'

'It's not African or Africana. They're Zulus,' responded Mairi-

Clare. 'They've been going for years, but with the ban because of apartheid no one has really heard of them ... well, apart from Terence.'

'Even worse ... how the hell can we replicate that? Crying out loud, Tubbs! Could ye no huv' went for Madness or Spandau Ballet or something?' Mikey exclaimed, seeking to reaffirm his position in the group hierarchy.

Tubbs slowly made his way to the bay window. Wiping the condensation with the back of his hand, he peered out onto the grimy weathered sandstone. It dominated the landscape and competed with the black slate roofs as the most depressing urban feature even on the sunniest of days. After summer showers, when the sun emerged through the ageing sash windows to soak up the moisture and glisten once again, he would sit and sketch from his bedroom window. The solitude cleared his mind; art was his favourite subject and by far his most engrossing pastime. One day, he promised himself, he would travel the world taking in all the great galleries wherever they were; maybe his works would adorn their walls. He had never set foot outside Paisley, with the exception of two weeks on holiday in Millport. He knew there was a great big, exciting, world out there awaiting his company. Somehow he would get there to experience it.

'Look, ah'm fat as fuck. Ah cannae sing. Ah cannae play any instruments but Ah kin dance!' Tubbs bemoaned. 'Huv ye seen they Africans dancing doon the street?' he added, in an impassioned voice, whilst pointing towards the Panasonic record player in the corner. 'Facing they racist polis with sticks, 'n' getting' shot wae bullets? Dancing, fucking dancing, facing up tae that. We kin dae' that. *Ah* kin dae' that!' he exclaimed, slumping on the window ledge, his eyes fixed on the patterned carpet'

Mairi-Clare glanced at Mikey, waiting for him to take the lead and support his friend. Typically, the West End boy was not in tune with emotional attainment.

'Terence,' she spoke softly as she moved across the room to face him. 'Don't worry about not playing an instrument. You'll carry out perfectly what I have in mind.' She wiped the tousled hair from his face and raised his chin to face her. *Why did I do that?* she thought as her body froze for a second.

Recovering and moving towards the stereo she added, 'Listen to this music. If you are really wanting out of this town this is your route to travel the world ... classical music. Trust me.'

'Jesus Christ,' muttered Tubbs, shuffling his feet.

In the other room, Dixie tugged at his friend's arm and pulled him towards the table and chairs. 'Ye cannae work fur him, Peter. Awright, I do a bit of maintenance fur him and they seem tae trust me, but I'm no' *dealing* wae him. It's cash in hand and see ye later. Trust me, some of the half-conversations I've heard! Thank God ah never hear the full script.' Dixie became animated as he moved around the kitchen.

'Dixie, I've got mouths tae feed, same as you. Christ's sake, I've got fuck all, not a bit of food in the fridge, kids can't go oan any school trips or have half-decent gear. Best thing about school is they get a free lunch, fuck's sake! Mikey's wearing cast offs from oor Barry's weans in Canada. This is nae way tae live.'

'He's just worried, Peter. Everyone knows what Quinn's like, bloody evil,' Grace interjected, rubbing her friend's arm.

'I know, Grace, but if ah go tae work for him I'll just do ma shift, keep ma heid doon and earn some cash,' Peter replied reassuringly.

'I know ye will. Just take care – and take them two fillet steaks in the fridge up the road with ye. They'll be wasted on him the morra when he's lying aboot with a massive bloody hangover.'

'Don't worry, I'll be fine. And yer right, they would be wasted oan him,' Peter responded, wrapping his arms round her shoulders and placing a kiss on her forehead. 'I'll have a think about it. Ye never know, Ah might win Spot the Ball,' he laughed. 'Right, I'm off. Mikey, see you back at the house,' he called out, punching Dixie on the back of the head as he left the room.

'Well that wis different,' said Tubbs, looking towards Mikey after listening to all fourteen minutes forty-three seconds of the absorbing symphony.

'*Capriccio Italien*. Tchaikovsky wrote it after coming across a carnival in Rome and being inspired by the atmosphere and whole show being played out in front of his eyes. It's all about fun and love. The trumpet crescendo introduction heralds the start of the event. However, like all good tales there are dips and high points. There are eighteen instruments in that one piece alone,' Mairi-Clare said confidently, becoming animated with unbridled enthusiasm. 'I guarantee I can find one for everyone.'

Mairi-Clare had fallen in love with classical music and Tchaikovsky in particular while learning the violin. In her previous life, when money was no object, her parents paid for piano and string instrument lessons twice per week. She settled on and excelled with the violin and the classical forms. The consistent ebb and flows of Tchaikovsky's music in particular captivated her as the mesmerising, evocative, sounds allowed her to block out all that was happening around her and become engrossed in the moment. Every note of Capriccio Italien was embedded in Mairi-Clare's mind. She would pass on her knowledge to her new friends, who knew where it may lead.

'What you think Mikey?' Tubbs asked in an uncertain tone.

'Well, I...'

'Sorry, I need to go,' Mairi-Clare interrupted, grabbing Mikey's wrist to scan his silver Casio timepiece, 'I've got my school partner for the St Mary's special Mass coming round.'

'But whit about Mikey's choice? We've still tae hear it.'

'Mikey, I'm really sorry,' she responded, widening her eyes and flirting gently with him.

'No probs. Ah wis just gonnae dae Francois Chopin anyway.'

'Do they no smash up instruments?'

'So we're gaun' for this orchestra thing?' Mikey responded.

The nervous nodding confirmed it.

'Not a word in school, agreed? Or we'll get our baws well and truly booted,' Tubbs added worryingly.

'Good choice, Mikey. We'll arrange to come to mine after school. We can work it out then,' Mairi-Clare replied quickly as she rushed out of the door.

Chapter Seven

CAL LOWERED HIS HEAD and fixed his eyes on his notes. Biting the inside of his gum to circumvent his sniggers, he gathered his thoughts so he could advise his potential new client.

'So, that's the lot, boss. Awright, hands up, Ah shouldna huv done it and Ah should know better, but she owed me. I'm no' a feckin charity.' Dixie was becoming agitated as he briefed his new lawyer on his exploits at Calside Avenue.

'Mr Clark, have you been charged with any offence?'

'No' yet, but Ah will be. It's a certainty, and please call me Dixie. Look, Ah cannae go tae jail but Ah'm no paying that Fitzgerald a penny. But Ah don't want tae see Swimmer in court either. Ah know it wisnae wise, but it was spur of the moment stuff.'

Dixie was now out of the seat, running his hands through his greying hair and transferring his weight from one foot to the other; this was his natural reaction to any stressful situation. He suddenly remembered his childhood, standing in front of the children's panel, shifting his feet incessantly, promising with all his heart to attend school and stop stealing lead from the roofs of the new building sites around the West End.

'Please sit down, Mr Clark. Please, Dixie ... sit.' Cal's voice was reassuring. That, together with maintaining continuous eye contact, ensured he remained in control of discussions. He had done this on numerous occasions; he knew that no case file would be created with a ranting client. 'I'll check with the procurator fiscal and Mill Street to ascertain if Mr Christie – Swimmer – was charged with any offence or attended the station.'

'Thanks a million, Mr Lynch. Look, about paying ye. Ah don't want legal aid. They'll check my accounts for ma business, and that Ah don't want.'

'Well, let's wait until I get more detail, shall we?' Cal replied sharply.

'Ah was thinking, yer new in these parts, eh? Ah could give ye a guided tour. Ah know everyone, most of their business, and just aboot all the gossip. I could point out potential new clients.' Dixie's yellow teeth protruded through his smirk.

'Oh, the clients will come. But thanks for the offer.' Cal rose from the seat to direct his visitor to the door.

'Has Eddie Quinn been tae see ye yet?'

Cal tried to hide his surprise as he stalled at the partially open door. 'Eddie Quinn? That name sounds familiar from the old files I've read,' he answered cautiously.

'Should be. This was where he done business. Had the last guy in his pocket, trying to keep the polis at bay for him. Look, I'll take ye for a walk, no harm done. How's 'bout the morra lunchtime? Okay, good. See ye then.' Dixie moved swiftly out of the office door.

'Two things, Dixie,' Cal responded. 'First, provide a cost for the maintenance work from the list Ms Knox will provide. That may assist with any fees. Secondly, you've forgotten to take your boy.' He pointed at Terence, who was engrossed in Cal's record collection.

'Crying out loud, Terence move yersel'! And ye better not have blagged any of this man's gear,' Dixie shouted.

Terence turned, startled but enthused. 'Mr Lynch, cool collection. Very impressive, especially the classics. Could ah borrow this wan?' he asked, raising Tchaikovsky's classic symphonises aloft. 'See, Ah'm in a band – well, an orchestra – well, no yet, but we're gonnae be an orchestra. Ah need tae learn one of these tunes. We've no' got any instruments, yet. But we're getting them, Ah think. It's complicated,' he sighed, frustratedly spinning the album between his palms. 'I'll bring it back, promise, and listening tae the auld man, it's no' as if we won't be visiting ye ever again,' he added.

'You tell yer mother anything about this, wee man, and you'll not see the week out never mind playing that poncey music,' Dixie replied through gritted teeth.

'Of course you can borrow it, Terence,' Cal said. 'Keep me updated with your progress. It's great to hear of young people being interested in the classics. Tell me, do you have a younger brother?

'Two. The one you're interested in, Joe, he's been making money out of this place fur months. To be fair, Ah dae think the junkies woulda rattled the office if him 'n' Shada weren't hinging about like a bad smell,' Terence laughed.

'Well, could you tell him his efficient services are no longer required? Or maybe your dad could tell him? Encourage him to go to school?' Cal raised his eyebrows to garner a response.

'Nothing to do wae' me,' Dixie retorted, dismissively. 'That's his mother's lookout. Right, let's go, Terence. An' ta, Mr Lynch. Honestly, if ye clear this wan up, I'll always be in yer debt. Don't worry, I'll speak tae oor Joe.' He shook Cal's hand firmly. 'Catch ye the morra – half twelve?'

'That'll be fine, thank you. Have a nice day,' Cal responded, his thoughts turned to Dixie's throwaway comment.

Hopefully tomorrow his new acquaintance would provide more detail. If Cal felt it would be worthwhile, he would develop and manipulate the relationship for his own ends.

Chapter Eight

MAIRI-CLARE GREW INCREASINGLY contented with her new surroundings. School had settled down and she was absorbed in working with her 'Mass partner', Mary, and the hymn they had chosen to recite.

Her biggest surprise had been how drawn she was to Tubbs. The two were constant companions outside St Saviours, spending time sitting on the dyke outside her close or walking to Maxwellton Park to work the weather-worn swings, the rusted bolts screeching with each movement. What was the attraction? Maybe it was his vulnerability and openness, or the fact that they were comfortable sitting in silence as the world passed by. The only interruption was the old men clacking bowls beyond the large sandstone wall of the adjacent bowling green. Tubbs' deep, dark eyes seemed to draw her in and mesmerise her. Would he ever ask her out?

One day, she broached the issue of girlfriends. Tubbs shrugged. 'I usually leave all that kind a' stuff tae Mikey.'

Her Mass partner was equally intriguing. As an only child, Mary had a defiance that bordered on rudeness and bitterness towards life in general which, she learned, emanated from the premature death of her father four years earlier. Her initial meeting with Mairi-Clare had been tense, with Mary declaring her input would be minimal. God, if he existed at all, had been evil to rob her of her father.

'I'm only here to stop my mum nagging at me to take part in this useless event,' she said through gritted teeth, her eyes smothered by her lowered eyebrows.

* * *

'I'll get it,' Mairi-Clare announced, as the doorbell sounded.

Tubbs and Mikey were attending the inaugural meeting of the fledgling group. Joe and Shada, despondent with the preferred choice of music, had decided to stick to their various entrepreneurial activities around the town.

'Come in. Down the hall, last door on the right, that's my room. I'll get some juice.'

'I'm in her bedroom already, Tubsy boy,' Mikey sniggered.

Music blared from beyond a dark oak door. It had been left open, revealing a tall, scrawny male dancing in front of a full-size mirror wearing nothing but yellow Y-fronts and a pair of fur-lined tucker boots.

Mikey and Tubbs stopped, momentarily stunned. The male, his blond hair tied back in a ponytail, was on all fours as he pointed to an imaginary crowd. Simple Minds boomed as he mimed and gyrated around the room, overlooked by posters of Fidel Castro, statesman-like in his army fatigues, a helmet-clad miner pleading *Coal not Dole*, and the Rainbow Warrior heading out to sea to take on the latest multi-conglomerate.

The youth calmly glided towards the door and assessed the two visitors. His wide eyes eying them up and down. 'Bet you wish you could move like me, brothers. Peace,' he said quietly, then slammed the door shut in their faces.

'You've met my brother, then? Paisley's answer to Bono – or is it Jim

Kerr? Can't remember,' Mairi-Clare quipped, leading her friends to her room.

'So, we've agreed on classical music and we'll all learn an instrument for one piece, *Capriccio Italien*, and try out for orchestras. Mikey, you'll learn the orchestral flute – my dad has an old one. There are three flute players in this piece, so any mistakes you make won't be picked up. I'll join the strings and play the violin. Terence, you'll learn the bass drum.'

'She's quite bossy, Tubbs eh?' Mikey said.

'Typical, the fat guy plays the big drum. Good job I'm at one with my weight. And where am Ah going tae get a bass drum?' Tubbs smirked.

'Come here.' Mairi-Clare clutched his hand and led him to the large bay window. Mikey followed. 'Up there.' She pointed towards Case Road Orange Lodge, a large detached, red-sandstone building, which dominated the brow of a hill and sat at the crossroads of the two streets,

'The Protestant Boys Memorial Flute Band, I think they're called. They walk from there every Saturday without fail in the summer. We'll steal it for you,' she said assertively.

'Aw aye, Ah kin see that happening, nae bother,' Tubbs responded, moving away from the window as if to protect himself from the danger he imagined would be forthcoming, while raising his eyebrows and glancing toward Mikey.

'Jesus Christ,' Mikey laughed. 'Yer mental, hen! They'll leather us from one end of the toon to the next. Ye don't know these folk, dae ye?'

Mairi-Clare paused, fixing her glare on Mikey. 'I've a plan and I've been watching that building and that band right through the summer, both morning and evening. I had no choice – they woke me up every bloody Saturday without fail. After you asked me to join your merry musical band and we chose classical, it seemed the natural choice. They're creatures of habit, are usually under the influence by the time they come home around 5pm and, from what I've observed, easily manipulated. And Mikey, don't call me hen,' she hissed.

'Look, just keep listening to the music and think about your instrument. There are easy-to-learn books you can pick up in the library. I'll simplify the notes for you and give you timings for when you play during the piece,' she went on, walking between her friends. 'Two weeks' time, we take the drum. I understand they're playing at some anniversary event in Carluke, so they'll arrive back even drunker than usual. This weekend I'll triple-check the plan. I believe there's some sort of function on at Troon, so it will be a dry run.'

'Mairi-Clare, Ah'm no sure 'bout this. Seriously, that is … err … serious,' Tubbs whispered, rubbing her shoulder. 'If ye know what Ah mean.'

'Ye seem to have good sources but I agree with Tubbs. It's well dodgy,' Mikey piped up, feeling isolated.

'I get that, boys, but I've come up with a plan which will work, trust me. Terence needs a bass drum. None of us can afford even a second-hand one. They have one, a beautiful piece I should add.' She moved towards the stereo, reasserting her control. 'For now, we listen to the *Capriccio Italien.*'

'Can Ah no' play the tambourine?' Tubbs pleaded.

'No.'

'Say yer prayers, mate,' Mikey grimaced.

Mairi-Clare rang the bell of the top-floor flat at 10 Tweed Street. The close, which was in darkness, the lights subject to neglect, reeking of urine and stale air. Only one family occupied the building. All the adjacent and parallel tenements were vacant, derelict, and victims to scavenging for scrap metal and roofing lead. Sun-bleached floral curtains fluttered in the evening breeze through the broken windows, while metal doors prevented any unauthorised entry.

This would be her third session with Mary and gradually, tentatively, the barriers seemed to be receding.

A small, middle-aged, woman answered the door and beckoned her inside. 'You must be Mairi-Clare. Very pleased to meet you. I'm Diane, Mary's mum. She's in her room just now – we'll have a quick chat then you can join her down there.' She said in a thick Irish accent, directing her into the living room.

'Please take a seat, Mairi-Clare. Such a lovely name.'

Diane settled her soft eyes on her visitor. The room was the opposite to the external surroundings: warm and welcoming with a touch of opulence. Thankfully, it lacked the garishness Mairi-Clare had witnessed at some of her old school friends' homes in Kilmacolm.

'I want to thank you for helping Mary, and for your patience. I wish she would get out more. I assume you know about her dad. She hasn't got over it yet. I don't think she ever will. She blames me, blames the world, the good Lord and sometimes her dad himself, God rest him. I realise it won't be easy working with her but if she can free her mind, I think you'll discover a lovely person and maybe a friend. Mary would like...'

'Sorry, Mrs Cassidy, could you be quiet?' Mairi-Clare interjected sheepishly, pointing to the living-room entrance while tilting her head to hear more clearly. A young girl's voice was echoing throughout the flat. The mellifluous, weightless tones were delivered with a precision that prompted Mairi-Clare's rude interruption.

'That's Mary,' Diane whispered, smiling proudly and leaning toward Mairi-Clare. 'She only sings in her room. She sang constantly before Billy died. He would sing to her every day and each night when he put her to bed. He was from County Cork, a wee place called Reenascreena. Wouldn't imagine you'd have heard of it. They say the Cork folk sing when they talk and he had a beautiful lilt. He never really settled here, so he sang songs from home, to Mary. She's a great singer too. She doesn't get it from me because I can't sing a note,' she added, half smiling. 'I'll let her know you're here. Don't tell her you heard her sing – she'll just get upset,' she added, moving slowly towards the door.

'Hi, Mary, how are you doing?' Mairi-Clare queried as she entered the bright bedroom decorated in pink, with boy-band posters positioned high on all the walls. 'I've brought my guitar so we can practise the hymn, then maybe head up to the Big Apple for a game of pool. What you think?' She smiled and sat on the edge of the quilted bedcover.

'Sounds great,' Mary replied dismissively. 'Have you ever looked at this street?' She continued to peer through the Venetian blinds covering the window. 'Look at it. The place is a midden. That empty close across the road number fifty-nine – all sorts goes on in there. I don't miss anything. Nothing else to do in this dump.'

'You may be right, girl, but we have a song to learn. Here's your tambourine. Have I still to strum the guitar and do all the singing?' Mairi-Clare asked, nudging Mary's shoulder.

'Why do I have to go to a *special* school? I don't want to be fuckin' *special*,' Mary announced in a low tone.

Mairi-Clare was unclear whether she was actually engaging with her or just talking aloud to herself.

'We're not special but different, eh?' Mary faced her companion, her expression full of frustration. 'That's what it is, they can't *do* different 'cause my eyes are puffy, my voice croaky. It's not as if we're thick. Gavin Corr can recite poetry off by heart, and Skye Munro can do algebra and has a boyfriend, the wee cow.' She giggled. 'I used to sing, told I was good.'

At last, a breakthrough, Mairi-Clare thought.

'So why the *special* school?' she repeated. 'Scared in case we get called mongos, protecting us? Protecting the *normal* kids, more like. Wouldn't want them feeling uncomfortable round us, would they?' She turned toward the window again, despondently, awaiting a response.

'Well, maybe this Mass will be the start of it. It'll showcase all our talents. Let them see we're all the same – just different. Then we might all end up together in the one school,' Mairi-Clare suggested, gently poking her friend's ribs. 'Showing talent... Not just hitting a bloody tambourine eh?'

'No, not a chance,' Mary responded assertively.

Chapter Nine

'YOUR TWELVE-THIRTY HAS arrived, Mr Lynch,' Ms Knox announced via the intercom.

Cal grabbed his charcoal, pure-wool coat and placed it over his broad shoulders as he left the office.

'Aw, yer joking, man. Ye look like CID!'

'Well, as you stated previously, Dixie, you know everyone in the town, so not only can you introduce me but you can put them right. Lead the way,' Cal replied, wrapping his silk paisley-patterned scarf around his neck to counter the biting early November wind.

Dixie guided his new acquaintance along the narrow pavements. The noise of the buses and cars made conversation challenging. Stopping Cal in his tracks, he advised, 'Right, we'll walk up the West End 'n' I'll let you know the main players and the general gossip. Just as if we're out for a stroll or oan our way tae the pub. If we stop, or if Ah'm telling ye about a place, Ah won't be pointing. I'll either move ma heid or point ma toes towards it. Quinn's got eyes and ears everywhere, so we need tae be discreet or the jungle drums will start beating before you can warm yer seat with yer designer gear arse.'

Zipping his paint-stained canvas coat to below his chin, Dixie led the way at a brisk pace towards the West End cross formerly the retail heartbeat of the area.

A young girl grabbed Dixie's arm as they passed on the tight footpath. Smiling broadly she said, 'Hey, Dixie. Thanks for fixing my mum's sink. Really appreciate it.'

'No problem, pal.' He smiled broadly and continued walking. 'This place has some history, by the way. Folk forget that,' he announced, raising his arms in a welcoming fashion. 'Back in the day, this was the hub for revolution with the weavers - they took no shite. And did Ah no read somewhere of that character Disraeli saying "keep your eye on Paisley"? Aye, the West End, more like. That's the Co-op, arseholes think that's whit will save the place after they shut Chrysler and the Mills. How fuckin' stupid, eh? A fucking supermarket' he grimaced. 'Right,' he held Cal's forearm, 'haud it here.'

Leaning against the red breeze-block wall of the shop, he motioned Cal to do the same.

'Across the road beside the public bogs is the Thistle Bar, owned by Quinn. Above the Thistle is the office where he runs his business empire and plots to stay ahead of the polis. I dae some work for him for time tae time, jist general maintenance, remember Ah'm no' involved in any of his shite. Let's keep walking.'

Cal glanced across the busy road at the large blonde, sandstone building with a large, gold rimmed, ornate clock tower, at its apex, that dominated the West End cross, his eyes straining towards Quinn's office location. He wanted to ask the thousand questions swirling round his head, but he feigned interest in Dixie's revelations and, superficially, remained underwhelmed.

'Every shop...' Dixie continued.

A middle-aged woman interrupted. 'Dixie, will you pop up to ma da's soon? He needs some handrails put in. Won't let the Council do it, says it has to be you.'

'No probs, Sandra. Tell yer da I'll be up first thing tomorrow.'

'Thanks, Dixie, yer a star.'

'You are popular, aren't you?' Cal said.

'As I was saying, all these shops in the West End pay Quinn protection. Ah think it's only a couple of quid a week. It's more tae dae with his guys having a good reason tae visit the premises tae keep tabs oan folk 'n' getting intelligence oan any polis enquiries. Taxi office, beside Jack Ross the newsagents over there. That's his as well. Rumour is it's a front tae transport smack around the toon.'

'Nice contributor to the community, then?' Cal interjected nonchalantly.

'Aye, but he covers himself well. Sponsors the local weans fitba' team and paid for an incubator for the baby-care unit. He's untouchable. But don't think I'm a tout, it's jist you'll be working for him soon, guaranteed.' Dixie glanced ominously towards Cal as he continued to dander up the street.

'This shop we're gonnae pass, New Images, his daughter Suzie runs it. She takes hee-haw tae dae with him. Hates him, and they haven't spoken in years.'

'Any reason?'

'Don't know. She won't even use his surname. She seems half-decent and gives the young lassies Saturday jobs 'n' that. Think I'll go in sometime, get ma nails done.'

Cal peered in the large, full-wall window of the busy salon. Several women sat reading glossy magazines, their heads encased in some sort of contraption. A slim, tall woman spoke to a customer; her hands rested on the client's shoulders as she communicated via a large mirror. Cal caught her sharp, light-blue eyes and they locked for what seemed like forever. She smiled, her large red lips parting slightly as she tucked a rogue strand of her long black locks behind her ear.

'Aye, that's Suzie – and that's Swimmer's maw across the road. If she sees me, I'm fucking deid. Speed it up a bit.' Dixie moved his companion along, placing his hand on Cal's broad back while maintaining his gaze on Irene Christie.

'DIXIE, I'm going to slaughter you!' The female voice, shrill with aggression, startled Cal.

'Your, bright, shining star seems to be falling rapidly,' he smirked.

'Quick, cut doon through the Gallow Green. We'll sneak into the Vatican for a beer. She'll no' see us.' Dixie guided them along Broomlands and down the sharp turn onto Queen St, constantly looking over his shoulder as his pursuer tried in vain to navigate a break in the traffic.

'Garrotted seven witches here years ago,' he added, as they walked briskly through a small, unkempt grass area. 'Ah wish they'd bring it back for that nutcase before she gets me.'

* * *

Cal settled into a green, worn-leather seat in the ornate lounge. The pub was empty apart from a couple of old men hugging pint glasses in a booth, deeply engrossed in a game of chess, and a large bald man dressed in camouflage garb who was shuffling his feet on the worn floorboards to the Eurythmics blasting out from a modern jukebox, which was at odds with the stained-oak, Victorian interior.

'There ye go, best pint of Guinness in Paisley.' Dixie placed the two pints on the cast-iron table. 'Don't worry 'bout him. That's big Davie, he's in the TA – ye know, the weekend soldiers. He missed the shout for the Falklands war in '82. Daft eejit was away fishing at Loch Awe. Got steaming and missed the phone call.' Dixie glanced over his shoulder, smiling to himself. 'That's why he cuts aboot wae aw his camouflage gear oan and carries aw that army kit wae him. He disnae want tae miss another fight. Works for the council, even cuts the grass with aw that oan. Nutjob.' He called to the man, 'Davie, how's it gaun, big man? C'mon and meet ma mate, Cal.'

Davie waddled over, a pint and packet of salted nuts in hand. 'Nice tae meet ye.' He nodded, his mouth loaded with peanuts.

'Where's the next big fight then, Davie boy? See yer ready for it anyhow.' Dixie smirked, winking at Cal.

'South America, Dixie. Ah've a pal high up in the US Marines, done manoeuvres with him in Skye. Nicaragua, place is called. The commies have taken over. We'll go in and support our American comrades.'

'Were the Sandinistas not legitimately elected, with sixty-seven percent of the vote in Nicaragua?' Cal interjected, sipping and hiding behind his Guinness.

'Eh, aye but they're commies ...I think.' Big Davie was squirming and beginning to retreat to the bar.

'Yer quite brainy, eh, Mr Lynch?' Dixie enquired.

'The *Campesinos*, the farmers, have set up co-operatives all over the country. They took the land off the rogue landlords. For the first time, they are being educated, reading, writing, supporting their communities. I think that's what scares Davie's US friends – power to the little man.'

'That's all above ma heid.'

Cal laughed heartily, beginning to settle into his surroundings. 'Why the Vatican?'

'That's what it's called – or the Buddies, 'cause that's what it says above the door. If yer ever looking for me, just leave a message in here. I'll pick it up,' Dixie responded.

'Tell me, this guy Quinn. You say he's the most prominent businessman in the West End? How did he get that accolade?' Cal asked.

'Yer mate, the guy who works for ye – Joyce? He's in the Thistle many a lunchtime. Keeps himself quiet, just sits and does a crossword. He not told ye?' Dixie gulped his pint licking his upper lip while replacing the glass on the table, his eyes firmly on Cal.

'So you want to know about Quinn? Where ye fae? Whit 'bout Swimmer, is he getting charged? Whit 'bout me? Dae Ah need tae pay ye? Oh, and by the way, cheers for giving the boy that LP yesterday. Aw bloody night Ah haud tae listen tae it, plus Ah know aw 'bout this character Tchaikovsky. He wis arguing wae me this morning 'bout the merits of his music and folk saying it – lacked elevated thought. Seriously, though, he thinks it'll let him see the world when he joins an orchestra.'

Cal smiled. 'He may have a future with music, then. Just try and encourage him. And too many questions in one breath.' He looked around the pub. 'Does this place do lunches?'

'Aye, ready salted or cheese 'n' onion.'

'I was born and raised in Glasgow, the Gorbals, but spent my formative years in London. That's where I trained at the Bar. You will not be charged, nor will your friend. Not in the public interest. But buy that woman a door or you might be. So, Quinn?' Cal asked, attempting to cloak his impatience.

Dixie looked over both shoulders, leaned forward and spoke in hushed tones.

'I don't know how he does it. It's as if he's untouchable. Polis have never laid a glove oan him – always avoids a charge. He runs aw the drugs in and out of the toon, wi' scary henchmen doin' his dirty work fur him. He's got his fingers in every pie – protection rackets, security – and his taxi drivers are glorified crooks. Though ma mate's just starting wae them, but he's sound. Worst of all, Quinn has all the councillors licking his arse 'cause he's a fucking economic success story! They should be patting me and lovely Gracie oan the back for keeping the weans away fae his fucking smack.'

Cal feigned surprise; he was aware of most of the points Dixie raised but reinforcement was always worthwhile.

'There's nothing for the young wans here now, wae' aw the facto-ries shut. Only way they think to block it oot is through his gear. A read aboot it, happens wae the Native Americans and the Aborigines. See, if folk huv' nae hope or role models or decent jobs, that's when the scum step in to dull the hopelessness.'

Dixie leaned closer to Cal. 'Folk who have stood up tae him go missing. At least two Ah know of - never seen again,' he added, drawing his finger across his neck.

'And you reckon I'll be in his employ?' Cal grinned, regretting his choice of phrase too late.

'Money's money, pal. Just don't dae his dirty work and charge him plenty. One of his people is on trial soon – jist heard the brief's been bagged. You'll be asked, so be ready. Right that's enough the now. Ah need tae go and price a job. At least pretend you'll stay and finish that pint.' Dixie shook Cal's hand and left the pub, calling big Davie a plastic war hero as he escaped.

Cal strolled back towards the office, the cold air nipping his smooth skin. Being uncharacteristically disorganised when it came to food, and constantly eating on the go, meant he was now becoming a familiar face around the West Ends fast-food outlets, and he visited the Hippy Chippy to purchase his lunch, the smell of freshly cut frying chips enticing him in. The streets had quietened as he meandered onward, glancing repeatedly towards Quinn's office windows. He failed to notice the young woman carrying boxes from the salon.

'I'm really sorry! Let me help' he said, as she bent to lift the spillage.

'It's fine, no harm done. It's only paper certificates for the college students,' she replied softly, looking up from her crouched position on the pavement.

Cal recognised her striking features immediately. As she lifted the boxes towards her car, he joked, 'Here, let me help. All that lifting isn't good for you.'

'All those Hippy Chippies aren't good for you,' she replied sharply, her bright eyes darting towards his newspaper-wrapped lunch.

Throwing the boxes in the boot of a small car, she turned to face him. 'Hi, I'm Suzie McGrath. I run this wee salon. And you must be?' she enquired.

'Cal...'

'Lynch, the new lawyer,' she interjected. 'Whole West End's gossiping about you, especially the women. Now I've met you, I'm not too sure what all the fuss is about.' She smiled, mischievously eying Cal from top to toe.

'Yes, that's me,' he replied sheepishly, suddenly stuck for words.

'Well, nice *bumping* into you Mr Lynch,' she said, hurrying into the car.

'Can I buy you a drink or maybe dinner to make up for the *bump?*' he called out as she started the engine and moved away. He watched as she manoeuvred the car quickly onto the carriageway and sped away.

Suddenly the white reverse lights came on as it returned to its starting point.

'Yes, you can,' Suzie replied from the open window. 'But it won't be the Hippy Chippy. You free tonight?' she asked, tapping her manicured nails on the steering wheel.

'I am, actually.'

'Meet me here at 6pm. I have to attend an awards' ceremony for young people and then you can buy me dinner. Bye.' She smiled and Cal replicated the expression, though he did feel his was more of an infatuated gaze as the car sped off towards the traffic lights.

* * *

Cal awoke with a startle. The soft pillow he lay on was reverberating, he was sure of it. His head was pounding and he felt his tongue sticking to the roof of his mouth.

He tried to rewind his actions from the previous night. The evening had started in such a civilised manner with his attendance at the beauty salon graduate ceremony, hosted very professionally by Suzie. He had presented her with an understated bunch of flowers, which, he thought, were well received.

After the ceremony, they'd had a great evening sampling the food at a local Italian restaurant, where their conversation hadn't been stilted and they'd shared their love for good food and sharp clothing. After which, it all becomes a bit hazy though he did recall drinking whisky chasers.

He looked down and realised he had slept in his designer suit, which seemed to have absorbed some stains along the way. Slowly rising, he made his way to the kitchen, the early morning autumn sun piercing his eyes as it arrived uninvited thorough the large window. It was reflecting off the adjacent River Cart and that didn't help his fragility. What the hell had happened last night? Had he opened up to Suzie? Did she ask any telling questions – and had how had he reacted?

A Post-it note was attached to the white kitchen cupboard: *thanx for a great night never thought I'd have put you to bed, call in sometime – Suzie x.*

Cal looked at his reflection in the mirrored glass oven door. His skin grew ever more purple as his train of thought returned. He recalled Suzie waking him as the taxi arrived at his plush apartment and her guiding his staggering, drunk body up the two flights of stairs. It had been his first night out since opening the office and it had reinforced what he always knew –he couldn't handle drink. It had also exposed his vulnerability, which could potentially interfere with his ultimate goal. Last night had been enjoyable, he thought, but it would be the last time he wouldn't be in control, at least until his plan had been implemented.

A ringing phone pierced his thumping head. 'Hello, Cal Lynch,' he managed to squeeze out.

'Mr Lynch, Sergeant Telfer, Mill Street Police Station. I believe you're the duty solicitor this bright Saturday morning?'

'I am, sergeant.'

'We have a customer here seeking your services.'

'Okay, I'll be right there,' Cal responded.

'No rush, he's having his quality full-English breakfast at present. You have some strong coffee and sober up. We'll see you in an hour.'

'Goodbye, sergeant.'

Right: painkillers, shower, Mill Street and hopefully call in to Suzie at the salon, he thought, *and sheepishly apologise and try to put the missing pieces together from last night.*

The short walk along the River Cart helped clear his head and freshen his mind. The fast-flowing river meandered through the town and collided at the Hamills', causing a white foam that brightened the landscape against the dark imposing walls of the mill. He would call in to the florist on the way to Mill Street and order his mother some flowers. He never missed the first Monday of the month to remind her he was thinking of her. It had started at the age of eleven, when he'd rushed home from school in Camden Town and stolen bright blossoms from the few manicured gardens along the way to try to make her smile again.

Cathy Lynch had never settled in London though she'd vowed never to return to Scotland, where she had lost everything with the exception of her loving son.

Cal walked down the small gradient to Mill Street Police Station. It resembled similar public buildings throughout the country, with its unforgiving pre-cast concrete blocks, straight lines and lack of features, which made the tasks carried out inside even more depressing.

'Good afternoon. Cal Lynch, solicitor,' he announced, as he presented himself at the high desk to the uniformed officer.

The officer raised his head from his newspaper and removed his glasses to look at the visitor. The middle-aged man looked as if he had spent his whole life in the police force; he looked war weary, no doubt brought on by some of the sights he'd seen during his many years of service. 'Mr Lynch, welcome. I called you this morning. Please sign in. CID brought your client in last night. He'll be facing charges of house breaking, selling stolen goods, and resisting arrest, I believe,' he said, indifferently. 'I'll buzz you in the door to your left.'

Cal moved towards the door, his trusted, lucky, brown leather brief-case under his arm.

'Third door on the right down the corridor. Your client will be with you shortly,' The sergeant moved his large frame to the side to allow Cal to continue along the corridor.

'Sergeant Telfer.' He paused, turning to face the officer, 'How did you know I had a hangover this morning?' Cal asked curiously. The question stopped the sergeant in his tracks.

'Apologies, Mr Lynch. I assumed everyone in Paisley required a pick-me-up on a Saturday. You're clearly not from these parts,' he responded.

Cal was halfway down the narrow corridor when Telfer called, 'Mr Lynch, where are you from, as a matter of interest?'

'London, sergeant. Why do you ask?' he responded, cautiously.

'You look very familiar, but I don't know from where. Too many faces, too many years,' the sergeant replied, returning to his worksta-tion. 'Roll on retirement,' he murmured to himself.

The fluorescent lights irritated Cal's eyes as the remnants of the previous night continued to linger. His client, John Faulds, signed the legal aid papers and immediately asked Cal for a cigarette. Cal had learned long ago to keep a pack in his leather case. Clients were always more relaxed and forthcoming with information after a few long drags on a cheap cigarette.

John's ragged appearance was no doubt in keeping with his chaotic lifestyle. He smelled of dampness, his clothes covered in mud and grass stains and a freshly swollen right eye protruded through his long, matted hair.

'Right, John, you know the routine as you've been here on previous occasions, I believe. They have you on several charges and they may oppose bail,' Cal said with authority. 'No comment to all questions. Save it for court. And tell me what happened to your eye?'

'Aye, nae probs, boss. If they haud me, slip me some fags, will ye? My eye? Fell into a cop's size nine,' John replied cynically. He was still tired and sore from last night's exploits trying to avoid Strathclyde Police.

The interview room door opened with a creak and two suited officers entered.

'Good afternoon, Mr Lynch. Detective Sergeant Frank Lawrie and this is Detective Constable Jim Munro,' the tall, sharp-featured officer announced as he sat opposite Cal and his client. 'Shall we get started? This shouldn't take too long.' He quickly skimmed through a file. 'John will be charged with those offences cited on the charge sheet provided. We won't be seeking to remand him so our work here is done ... for today,' Lawrie advised, his eyes fixed on Cal.

Cal opened his file and primed his pen. 'You're not presenting any evidence or planning to ask my client questions today?'

'No.'

'So we will look forward to the opportunity to contest it in court.' He realised there was no valid reason for him to prolong the discussion, but he felt he had to lay a marker with the DS as they would no doubt cross swords in the future.

DS Lawrie lowered his head and placed his closed hand under his unshaven chin. 'Mr Lynch, I've known your client, young John here, since he was ten and I was in uniform chasing his rear end down the High Street as him and his mates went on shoplifting sprees. He knows the scoop. Once we go to court, he'll be getting at least a year in Barlinnie. If he pleads before it gets to the bench, he'll get a reduced sentence – unfortunately.' There was exasperation in his voice that signified his frustration with the system. 'We have evidence that John has done twenty-three houses across Paisley and reset hundreds or thousands of pounds worth of goods, so...'

'So present the evidence, detective. My client will be answering not guilty to all charges, so let's get on with it, shall we?'

John snorted. 'Have you two been demoted? Ah mean Ah'm no' up tae date wae the polis ranks 'n that, but are you two no' a bit overqualified tae be chasing hoose breakers? Alleged, of course.'

Munro straightened his back and glared in response as the comment hit a nerve.

'Ye see, I've got a wee theory, right? You two huv been left holding the fort wae' that fat desk sergeant oot there cos aw yer uniformed mates are away up at Bilston Glen or Ravenscraig, leathering the shite oota a poor striking miner, or mibbae even running amok doon in some pit village in Ayrshire. Would that be right? With thur fucking ID lapel numbers removed 'n' getting paid plenty for dain it, nae doubt. Adding tae the forty-five percent pay rise that yer mate Thatcher gave ye back in '79 tae dae her dirty work fur her.' He sneered, placing his legs on the edge of table.

'Mind yer mouth, ye wee fucker,' Munro hissed, swiping the feet to the floor.

'Careful officer. Once they bring in taped interviews, you'll no be able tae knock us aboot in here anymore. Ah heard that's oan the cards,' John replied, winking at his lawyer.

Lawrie placed a hand on his colleague's arm, signalling him to remain calm.

'Very observant of you, John. Still reading the *Socialist Worker* then? You should have stuck in at school instead of stealing from others. Anyway, in answer to your question, Mr Lynch, don't worry – there will be plenty of evidence that we will present to the fiscal,' Lawrie retorted, rising from the seat. 'No doubt I'll see you back in here again, Mr Lynch. Paisley lawyers do quite well out of this nick.' He strode out of the door, his companion following in his wake.

Chapter Ten

CAL STRAIGHTENED HIS RED silk tie. Good choice, he thought, authoritative but not overpowering. Though his nerves were beginning to show with moisture gathering in his armpits discolouring his tailored Savile Row shirt. No matter, his jacket would be staying on.

He sank into the soft leather sofa that seemed to consume him. Quinn's 'receptionist' stared at his visitor, while constantly picking at his gleaming white, gapped, teeth.

'Nails Lundie. I won't tell ye why he's called that. I just hope you don't see him in action,' Dixie had informed him ominously during one of their regular chats. He had fixed the meeting and was adamant that Quinn wouldn't turn up anywhere else. 'Always a controlled environment.'

The reception area walls were adorned with large framed certificates. Cal stood to find out more as the 'receptionist's' eyes burrowed into the back of his head: *A-Cabs - Employer of the Year, 1982; Paisley Chamber of Commerce; A-Securities – Best Practice in Customer Care; the Thistle Bar – Pub of the Year 1983.*

'Mr Lynch?' a curt voice asked from behind.

Keep calm, make it impersonal, business-like, and do not overreact. Cal turned to find a middle-aged, well-dressed man walking towards him, his feet sinking into the plush carpet. 'Eddie Quinn,' he announced, his hand outstretched.

'Cal Lynch.' He felt a large gold ring press against his skin as he took the hand.

'Please, join me.' Quinn guided him towards the office. 'No calls, Lundie.'

'Sure thing, boss.'

Cal's blood was running cold as his jaw tightened. Focus, focus, he told himself. He wandered round the room, scanning as he went.

The office followed the same mix of opulent grandeur and tackiness as the reception area. A large carved wooden desk dominated the centre of the room with plush, studded leather seats at opposite sides. The walls were dressed with framed pictures of Quinn with what seemed to be a variety of celebrities, handing over a cheque to NHS staff, a local football team with a new minibus, or receiving some business award.

He gets about, he thought.

'So you're the new brief in Wellmeadow?' Quinn said dryly, studying the paperwork on his desk.

Cal looked down and noticed his knuckles were white. His fists tightened as childhood memories returned, lonely times, confused years caused by the greying individual in front of him.

'Mr Lynch?'

'Sorry, Mr Quinn, it's been a long day already,' he responded, attempting to relax in the chair.

'The last incumbent stuck it out for a year – you look gubbed already,' Quinn stated grimly, raising his eyes, attempting to evaluate Cal's character.

'Oh, I'll be fine. I ran a very busy practice in East London. Once I have things running the way I plan, we'll be grand,' Cal asserted.

Quinn was now on his feet, moving towards the large ornate window, a slight limp noticeable on his left side.

'Jealously is a terrible trait, Cal. Can I call you Cal?' he asked, peering between the thick curtains to the street below. 'That and revenge. You agree? Of course you do.' It was a rhetorical question.

'You see, I'm successful.' His open palm steered Cal towards the numerous pictures on the walls. 'But there's always someone who wants to bring you down, isn't there?' He returned to his seat.

Where was this leading? Had Cal said too much to Suzie? Had she played him? He hurriedly scanned the pictures, seeking her glamourous presence.

He had called into the salon the afternoon after their first night out, and all seemed well. They'd been out on several occasions and his feelings for her were growing by the day. She never mentioned her estranged Dad.

Cal felt his mouth dry up, unable to respond. Maybe it was Joyce. He had not got any further forward with his employee's regular lunchtime visits to the Thistle Bar that Dixie had thrown into their first meeting.

'They have nothing on me because I'm nothing but a legitimate, successful businessman,' Quinn exclaimed. 'They've been at it for the past five years. So they try to attack me through my staff. I want you to take a case for me. It's all here.'

He slid a file across the desk and it landed on Cal's lap. 'Okay,' he replied weakly, trying to compose himself. 'I'll read it and get back to you.'

'Don't bother, just go through Lundie. He might look thick as fuck, but he knows what I want. And make sure you submit your invoices on time. I'll keep my eye on it from afar. Get a not guilty and there'll be more work coming your way. And a word of warning: I don't like failure and – how can I put it – any fucking surprises.'

Quinn controlled the meeting with his slightly threatening tone and alpha-male assertiveness.

Pick your words wisely, Cal thought. 'I'll get right on it and there will be no surprises,' he responded, glancing through the file as he rose from the seat. The meeting was concluded and small talk had been non-existent.

He wiped his face and neck with his hanky as he descended the spiral staircase into the autumn sun, the blue sky adding much-needed colour to the narrow lane to the rear of the Thistle bar.

Dixie was sitting on the bookmaker's wall opposite, sipping from a thermos cup, steam encompassing his weathered face. 'Well, how'd that go?' he asked, blowing on the contents of the cup. 'Ye want some? Home-made soup, its lovely but bloody roasting, though. Gracie made it.'

'It went well. Thanks for arranging it. Another new client,' Cal said, almost dismissively.

'Don't look up but ye must have made an impression. Quinn and that mad bastard Nails have their beady eyes on ye from the windae. Ye know, see since we were in school and Ah used tae rip the pish oot of that eejit Nails, he's never liked me.' Dixie spoke into the cup.

'Right, must get back to the office.' Cal buttoned his coat. 'Why don't you and Grace join me for dinner one night? You could tell me about your boy's orchestral ambitions.' He spoke as he walked, not fully engaging with Dixie and instantly feeling a wave of loathing for his own dismissive manner. As he turned, he saw that his friend had already gone.

'Aye, nae bother.' A voice came from the bookmaker's entrance. 'I'll speak to Gracie.'

Good planning and intensive research on all the local law firms and Quinn's traits had been beneficial. Quinn had routinely used the Wellmeadow practice for his business dealings. Maybe it was the high turnover of lawyers leading to the protection of his secrets, or it may be the location at the epicentre of his ruthless firm garishly dressed up as A-Associates, which allowed him to keep an ever-watchful eye on the unfortunate incumbent brief. Whatever the rationale, Cal was where he wanted – and more importantly planned – to be, located right in the middle of it all.

Chapter Eleven

MIKEY WAS NERVOUS AND agitated as he stood in the darkness awaiting the signal. 'This is nuts, Shada mate. We're gonnae get killed fae this mob, nothing surer. Ah'm shitting it here.'

Shada was impassive, focussed, staring straight ahead. 'Ah think it's a good plan. She's thought it oot well,' he responded confidently, pulling his skip hat low in an attempt to conceal his upper face.

They had assembled earlier in the evening in Mairi-Clare's bedroom to run over the plan once again.

'Do not concern yourself with what others are doing, just concentrate on your own role,' she asserted. A hand-drawn map of the area lay on the bed. 'Everything will run in sequence. Every action has a consequence. They will react as we anticipate, believe me. We will be done, dusted and out of there in no time at all.' Mairi-Clare scanned the conscripted group, exerting confidence. 'Questions?'

'Just one – what if it aw goes tits up, pardon ma language.'

'Well, if it does, Mikey, Terence will not have a drum. We can't practise any orchestral music and we'll all be fighting over the two checkout jobs that'll be on offer at the Co-op over the summer.'

'Well, if ye put it like that,' Mikey responded, sheepishly.

'The bus will return at 7.30 tonight from Carluke. They'll be seriously drunk, as expected. If they're not, it's off. Remember the signal is when I move towards the bus and then we go as we practised. Clear?'

'Ah'm fuckin' looking forward tae this,' Joe announced, bouncing up and down hyperactively. 'Me and Shada's takings are doon fae the Co-op trolleys every time they're oot banging aboot in the summer. Payback is sweet, eh, mate?'

Shada smiled.

The street was in near darkness, illuminated only by the tall amber streetlights. The moon, so bright merely an hour earlier, was now enshrouded in a blanket of black clouds as the headlights of the bus guided the driver round the sharp bend and to a stop at the brow of the hill and the Orange Hall.

A cacophony of harsh adult voices could be heard singing and shouting as the bus door opened. Staggering, some assisting their drunken brethren, the passengers negotiated the steps and the short walk to the front door of the impressive red sandstone building. The almost regal purple-and-gold sashes hanging proudly around their necks were entirely at odds with their accompanying, dishevelled clothing.

Mairi-Clare leaned against the wall, biding her time. Slowly but surely, the street returned to its previous quiet state. The diesel engine shut down and the driver was now on the street, opening the baggage hold. She watched as the rear of the bus opened to reveal the band's impressive drum equipment. Two members placed the kit on the pavement as the driver returned to his cab to make his way home.

'Excuse me, mister. Is that your red Ford Cortina down there?' Mairi-Clare spoke quickly as she approached the men, both of whom were worse for wear.

'Naw, young yin,' one replied, struggling to focus, his eyes smarting from the smoke rising from the cigarette burning in the side of his mouth. The stale smell of his breath made her turn her head away momentarily.

'Oh, Ah thought it was. Ma da's a member, John MacKillop. Just thought you were the Grand Master, 'cause it's his car. Ah know 'cause his wife took me and ma pal Jean, their daughter, tae Barshaw Park in it jist last week. Anyway doesnae matter. It's jist there are two boys tanning it jist now.'

'Whit? Where?'

'Doon there.' She pointed towards the sharp bend, beyond the sight line of the hall. On cue, Mikey and Shada emerged from behind the cherry trees and dropped a large metal bar noisily on the pavement to signal their presence near the pristine red Cortina.

'Hawl, ya wee bastards.' The two men moved towards the parked vehicles, attempting to gather speed though their intentions seemed to be working faster than their buckled legs.

Turning, the drunker of the two shouted, 'You watch they drums fur us, hen, tae we sort these wee fuckers oot.'

'Okay, will do.'

Four pristine snares and a large bass drum sat on the pavement, emblazoned with gaudy images of King William of Orange looking majestic on his white horse.

Mairi-Clare watched the two men as they staggered away from the hall towards the targeted car. She turned and nodded quickly towards the adjacent church wall. On cue, Tubbs and Joe emerged from the darkness and lifted the large bass, quickly retraced their steps through the church grounds and along the six-foot wall leading to Queen St and the pre-arranged hiding point of the Gallow Green.

The two vigilantes retreated towards the hall, staggering in their cheap slip-on shoes that seemed to touch every inch of the tarmac along the way.

'Wee bastards ran like fuck when they seen us. Dropped this nail bar. So ye were right – jist aboot tae steal the cassette player oot the Cortina. Where's the drum?'

'Oh, one of yer pals took it in,' Mairi-Clare answered confidently without missing a beat as a great hollow thud came from beyond the churchyard wall.

'Whit was that?' The two were already on edge.

'Don't know, I think it came from the hall. Your pals will be wondering where you are.' She spoke less convincingly now as she stood between the church and the inquisitive band members. The stale-breath guy brushed her aside and peered over the wall into the church garden, the high gable ends blocking the street light.

Tubbs was lying prostrate on top of the wall; he had tripped and dropped the drum, causing the crash. He held his breath and didn't dare to move out of pure fear.

A drunken voice from the doorway of the club called, 'Sandy, move yersel. The troops are shouting for the tunes.'

'Aye, okay,' Sandy responded, continuing to stare into the darkness. 'Help me get these drums in.'

Mairi-Clare moved slowly, increasing her pace once she felt she was out of sight. Tubbs and Joe had made their way safely to the Gallow Green and secreted the immaculate drum under dark tarpaulin among the overgrown bushes as planned.

'That went like clockwork! Well done, MC,' Joe whispered excitedly, as the group met at the rendezvous point, the third pool table to the rear of the Big Apple.

'Did anyone see you hide it?' Mairi-Clare responded.

'Naw, don't think so.'

'If they bampots weren't steaming, we'd be deid by now.' Mikey was still shaking, constantly watching the door, expecting the hordes to burst in at any time looking for the stolen equipment and the thieves.

Shada smirked.

'They were always going to be drunk,' Mairi-Clare interjected. 'We have it now, that's what matters. Move it to my house tonight at ten o'clock. The streets will be quiet before the pubs come out. Terence can thank us all once he makes timpani in a top orchestra.'

The boys shared confused glances.

'That'll be the principal timpani,' Tubbs grinned.

The group relaxed, glad they had all survived in one piece.

* * *

A mere three months after arriving from London, Cal had settled well and was beginning to make headway with his business. The dark November nights had arrived and he certainly noticed a coldness in the air in contrast to the mild weather he'd experienced in his formative years down south. His clientele and caseload consisted of the same small time crooks, drunken disorderly and assault charges, like a repetitive, unbroken, cycle. It was cases that kept the office busy but not in profit. He was also intrigued by some historic cases which were on file relating to a number of prisoners seeking grounds to appeal their convictions. Once he found time he would expand this aspect of the business, he thought.

'Meet me at the Porridge Bowl. That's at the top of the hill behind yer office. I'll be in a white Escort – don't be later than 1900 hours.'

Cal was intrigued by the late phone call as he locked up the office. He drove steadily up the steep hill towards Coats Observatory, his mind racing. He'd recognised the voice but couldn't place it. He would find out soon enough.

The car vibrated as it crossed the roughly laid Roman setts. A car's headlights flashed in front of him. Cal pulled up to its rear and made his way to the passenger door. 'You? Now I'm interested. This must be worth delaying my exciting Fray Bentos dinner for.'

'Take a seat.'

'You have my undivided attention, DS Lawrie.'

'Call me Frank. Look at that view. Beautiful, eh, Mr Lynch? See that building there, the Porridge Bowl. Some kind git built it years ago and set it up as a school.'

Cal turned to glance at the imposing, pythonic structure, its oval roof shining within strategically placed white lighting.

'John Neilson, I think his name was. The only way you got in there was if yer parents were deid or poor. Well-quoted back in the day it was, and the weans would have come fae down there.' Lawrie pointed towards the sprawling council estate enhanced by the rows of streetlights. 'Seems very peaceful, doesn't it? Just folk going about their business. Trying to look after their families. But amongst aw that,' he waved his fingers, the smoke from his burning cigarette filling the dashboard, 'there's scumbags punting drugs to weans, creating junkies desperate for the next high.'

'This local history lesson is certainly very interesting, Frank, but my meal-for-one is growing more appetising by the minute.'

'See, the type of guy that set up that school doesn't exist anymore. In today's Paisley, entrepreneurs are very different – mostly ruthless filth. You're now working for one of them: Quinn. Defending his henchman, I hear. I assume you know how dangerous that fucker is?' The greying detective stared intently.

'I'm a lawyer, Frank, which means I represent and defend those who require it.'

'Franny McGurn left that old shopkeeper for dead for refusing to pay protection money. Smashed skull, fractured eye socket and a broken nose. His nerves are shot tae shreds. Once the scars heal, he's heading for Dykebar mental hospital for the foreseeable future – the guy's fucked.'

'I'm very sorry to hear that, but why am I here?'

'Drop the case. I've got at least two missing people still on the books in the last year courtesy of McGurn, on Quinn's orders. You're well out of your depth. Stay clear,' Lawrie advised, menacingly.

'Again, I'm a lawyer. I represent...'

'See that's what I find strange, Cal. Aye, yer a brief but my friends in London tell me you worked for the *wee guy*. Built up a sterling reputation for helping low-level cons. Kept them out of jail where ye could. Rumour has it you even set up training programmes to help them. I've not seen any evidence or heard of you taking on cases from the gangster fraternity. Then ye land here... Why the change? Why ye going over to the dark side, eh?'

Cal appeared calm, though he suspected Lawrie could hear his heart pounding in the forced silence.

He had established a successful career in London developed by working his way up within a large criminal practice, followed by setting up on his own in the East End of London where poverty levels and unemployment were inevitably followed by petty crime and consequential violence. He had a credible success rate at court and an equally impressive role in preventing reoffending by assisting his clients to engage, meaningfully, with the rehabilitation services on offer.

'Upholding the rules of the Bar Standards Board is very dear to my heart,' he said, 'and so is paying the bills. Sometimes you have to take the work where you can. Look, I'm new to this area and have to establish my practice. If you have an issue with a certain individual and believe this is an organised crime business, surely there's enough expertise and resources within Strathclyde's finest to tackle it head on.'

'No bad, nice deflection. I'm not convinced, Cal. There's more to you than meets the eye. I'll give ye the benefit of the doubt for now but, believe me, I'll hound you out if you keep working for that bastard.' Lawrie turned to face Cal his eyes narrowed to emphasise his intent.

Cal met his glare. 'Frank, I will do my job to the best of my ability. If your team have done theirs, there'll be no holes in any evidence for me to exploit. I defend; you get a conviction if my client's guilty. That's the way it works, isn't it?'

'Fair enough. Nevertheless, I'll help ye out. Any wee scroat I huckle and is crying for a brief, I'll get you called in. Might stop you working for him'

'Every little helps. Thanks. Are we done?'

'I wouldn't mind staying in touch, just between you and me, you understand? I don't think yer in his pocket – yet. Quinn's got touts everywhere including within the polis, so it's good tae talk.'

'I'll be happy to. But let's be clear, I won't share client information on cases. That's sacrosanct.'

'I'll be in touch.' Lawrie stretched out his hand.

'I'll see you in court,' Cal answered. 'A week next Tuesday for Mr McGurn's trial.'

'Look forward to it. Bye.'

How much research had Lawrie actually carried out with his

contacts in London, Cal wondered. Had he delved deep into his background? He was sussing him out, assessing what he would face in court, scoping his credibility.

Cal decided he would keep talking to Lawrie, develop a mutual understanding; another potential relationship would do his plans no harm whatsoever.

Chapter Twelve

CAL SPUN THE VINYL in his hands. Listening to music in his sparse office helped his concentration and thinking process, though his team's disquiet meant he only increased the volume when they left of an evening and he continued to work.

'Jack, you've looked over Mr McGurn's case notes again. What grounds do we have for a not guilty?'

Jack attentively read his copy of the file. 'Not great, boss. They have two witnesses, one being the victim and the other a bit dubious, by my reckoning. But they have photographs showing swollen and grazed knuckles on Mr McGurn from when he was lifted, forensics from the scene, and statements from the police interviews with McGurn after he was scooped two days after the assault while boarding a London-bound train at Glasgow Central. The second Crown witness puts our client at the scene and says he: "*saw him smash the victim's head on the urinal several times, stamped on him once he fell. He then walked away saying 'I'll be in yer shop next week have yer money ready'*." This will be a tough one.'

'So there were only three of them in the public toilet?' Cal placed the needle on his chosen record, Whitesnake's 'Here I go again. The decibel level led Jack to raise his head from the file.

'Sorry, I'll turn it down.'

'His name's, err, David Dawson. He says: *"I entered the toilet and two men were already using the facilities. The person to my left walked behind me as I relieved myself and attacked the person on my right. I froze to the spot, frightened, as the bigger man I described earlier really started laying in to the older man, who was screaming in pain. There was blood everywhere. I'll never pass through the West End again."* Aw, he's traumatised.'

'I hear you frequent the Thistle bar at lunchtimes. Have you heard any gossip?' Cal asked.

Jack frowned, feeling his loyalty was being questioned by his new boss. 'Your newfound friend Dixie never misses a trick. I haven't, as it happens. Have you met Mr McGurn yet?' he added, quickly changing the subject.

'I have. Thoroughly unpleasant individual. Very intimidating. Grab your jacket and bring the file with you, we're going to the crime scene.' Cal was already out of his office door. 'Ms Knox, we're heading out. I'll be back in time for my 4pm.'

'Do I have to listen to that awful racket?' she replied contemptuously, nodding towards the record player.

'Feel free to change it to something more to your taste,'

'Where's McGurn?' Peter peered through the mirrored glass partition of the taxi office, which was laid out with second-hand furniture, littered with job receipts and stacked with radio handsets. The only thing that seemed to be dust free was the Chubb safe situated in the corner adjacent to the manager's desk.

Two staff members were sitting with their backs to the window, fielding calls and issuing tasks to drivers via the two-way radio. One of them removed the telephone headset and proceeded to apply moisturiser to her hands, still not raising her eyes to meet her newest employee. 'He's still away on extended leave. He should be back next week, I think. I'm the office manager, Peter. Any questions, come to me. You know that.'

'Well, if you're in charge, Michelle, don't be giving me any more fares like the last one. Ah don't give a shit what the others allow in their motors but I'm no' driving that round the town. You got that?' Peter spoke in a low tone, though the conversation was picked up by the handful of drivers idling around waiting for a fare or about to go on shift.

'I've not got a clue what you're on about Peter, but I'll put you on the hospital run if that would be more suitable.' Michelle was now making eye contact with Peter, studying him intently.

'You do that,' he replied, leaving the office. The silence followed him out of the door. A fellow driver was at his back as he made his way to his car, which was situated at the front of four identical vehicles outside the office.

'Here, big man, whit was that aw aboot? I'm no' long started and want tae steer clear of any bother,' the younger man said.

'Mind yer ain,' Peter replied brusquely, closing the driver's door behind him.

'Taxi 1 to base. Get me an intelligence report on a Peter Mulheron, new start at A-Cabs. IC1, approx. six foot four, brown short hair, grumpy bastard. Mibbae potential informer. Dig up some dirt I can use. I'm heading for a couple of hours kip. I'll do the nightshift, see what they're up to then.'

The young driver returned the small handset to his inside pocket, checked his mirrors again for prying eyes then drove off, giving Peter a friendly wave as he passed.

Taxiing was not Peter's thing. He preferred to be active, using his hands, creating, not stuck behind a wheel for up to thirteen hours a day. In the past three weeks, he had managed to clear his provident cheque debt and put some decent food on the table, so all was not bad. He hated working for Quinn and, worst of all, people knowing that he did.

The risk of being caught up in the illegal activity that might be emanating from the taxi office made him determined to find some other line of work if possible. He'd hoped to get some parts for his car, book the boat for Donegal for the holidays and give the kids some money for new gear. *That's the plan*, he thought. No need to sign off the dole just yet. *I will do six months, tops.*

He had just spent the morning driving some wannabe gangster around four housing schemes in Paisley delivering what he assumed were drugs and lifting money. Once was enough, he thought. That wouldn't be happening again.

* * *

'Right, Jack.' Cal spoke through his scarf, the pungent smell of stale urine making him boak. 'There's something not quite right with his statement.'

The Victorian public toilets were dark and unwelcoming. A recent coat of paint did nothing to eradicate the repellent odours emitting from the urinals. White tiles remained stained with the victims' blood, and the edge of a urinal showing what seemed to be the point of vicious impact. The area's reputation ensured only the bravest, the most desperate, or drunkest male would risk their life and utilise the facilities on offer.

'Can't see anything, boss. Seems straightforward.'

'Think about it.' Cal walked slowly, recreating the scene. 'You enter a toilet, there's already two guys pissing here at the urinals. And you go and stand in between them? That would not happen, Jack, it's not natural.' Cal scanned the area looking for answers. 'Any guy would just go to one of those empty cubicles, would they not?'

He pushed open the wooden cubicle door revealing magnolia-painted skimmed surfaces, the remnants of forensic blue dust still visible on the walls and the heavily stained toilet.

'Ye may have something. I'll go over Dawson's statement again.'

'We need the full forensic report – that's where they've left a hole.

I guarantee it. First day of trial is tomorrow. There's a chance, due to the severity of the assault, that the sheriff may refer the case to the high court, which wouldn't be good for us. So, no pressure with this one.'

'I'll get onto it. Now can we get out of this rancid shithole?'

Emerging from the dimly-lit basement, their eyes squinted to adjust to the bright afternoon sun as they both inhaled deep breaths of fresh air.

'So, you head back, Jack, and trawl the file,' Cal said. 'I'll be in shortly. If I miss you, leave what you've found on my desk.'

He had spotted Suzie outside her salon directly across from the public toilets, helping an elderly customer into a taxi. Her elegance dazzled in the sunshine; her long dark hair shimmering as it flowed over petite shoulders, complementing her figure-hugging red dress.

'Well, how are you, Miss McGrath?' he asked. They were comfortable enough to greet each other with a kiss. 'I've not seen you for about eight hours.' He smirked cheekily.

'I'm fine, Mr Lynch. I thought I left quietly. Your snoring was a sure sign you were sleeping,' she retorted, her eyes full of mischief. 'Should I be worried about you leaving a public toilet with another man? Anything you wish to share?'

'Just a case I'm working on for your loving father.' His eyes diverted to Quinn's office window.

'Charge him plenty. Interesting case, is it?' she asked, walking swiftly towards her shop door.

Cal ogled her hour-glass figure. 'One of his employees is up for serious assault. Nothing exciting.'

'Tell me more,' she teased, clutching his waist. 'Guilty or squeaky clean?'

'You never did tell me why you don't get on with your daddy. Oh, you fancy a hot date Friday next week? There's a special Mass at St Mary's Chapel. The first invite I've received to anything since I arrived in this lovely town,' he said excitedly.

'Don't get too carried away – all local businesses are invited. And yes, I will accompany you. You'd better get your rear end to confession beforehand.'

'Fancy dinner this Saturday evening? That lovely Italian where you got me drunk on red wine and malt whisky?'

'Go on then, pick me up at seven. You can tell me all about your court case. I have to go, Mrs Curtis might be frying under the dryer. And ... he's a violent scumbag, that's why I don't have anything to do with *him*.'

* * *

Peter tried to block out the mundane surroundings of the dole office. In a bid to avoid the embarrassment of meeting commuters heading to their shops and offices, for the last three years, he had always arrived at Smithill Street by 9am for signing on. Though he had worked from the age of fourteen and was clearly due every penny, the indignity of being on the bru, and the personal self-loathing he felt for failing to provide for his family, was something he couldn't eradicate.

High grey walls peppered with advisory posters that no one paid a blind bit of attention to, stained blue plastic chairs screwed to the floor, vagrants, drunks and the disenfranchised, led him to daydream of better times until his number was called to sign and he could escape back to the comparative reality of the street and take a wander along the riverbank. There he found some peace watching the heron guard its territory along the River Cart, its slim grey neck darting as it looked for prey.

'Mr Mulheron, you're here to present yourself for unemployment benefit. Are you actively seeking employment?' The officious staff member enquired from behind the security glass as she studied Peter's dole card.

'Every fortnight, Mrs Jacobs, you ask me that and the answer is always the same – I'm currently available for, and actively seeking, employment. Dying to work.' He laughed, tapping his fingers impatiently on the counter. The charade was becoming tiresome but he knew he would be out soon enough.

She lifted her eyes toward the glass, the first time they had met his in three years. 'Mr Mulheron, go to room two, please. My colleague would like to discuss your claim.'

'Eh, what's this all about?'

Her outstretched hand directed him to a door at the rear of the office.

Peter entered the room as two individuals arrived via a door on the other side of an excessively wide table. He assumed the width of the furniture provided a safety buffer for staff being subject to attack by their disgruntled clientele. The large red panic button added to the unreceptive environment.

'Mr Mulheron, take a seat, please.' The staff member had his creased shirt sleeves rolled up and his tie hung untidily around his neck, protruding over his inflated waist.

'What's the problem?' Peter enquired, trying to sound assertive while eyeballing the untidy staff member and his female colleague. She seemed the meeker of the two; her head was bowed and her stare fixed on a closed brown file. If things got bad for him, he would concentrate on her.

'Mr Mulheron, just a couple of cross-checks. You reside at 29 George Street and are currently claiming unemployment benefit?' The man's nasal voice was monotonous, something he had clearly worked on no doubt to appear as bureaucratic and impervious as possible.

'Correct. Now what's the problem?'

Mr Untidy opened a small brown file and sighed. 'Mr Mulheron, we have evidence that you have been participating in paid employment while still claiming benefit from the state which, as we believe you are working, is not due to you. If you wish, I can show you photographic evidence of you engaged in paid employment with a company called A-Cabs Limited.'

Caught red-handed, Peter fought to control his rising temper. 'Ye know, Ah've done some shitty jobs in my time, but Ah couldnae do yours. How'd you sleep at night?' He glanced at the petite woman to garner sympathy, but her eyes remained fixed on the pictures being placed on the Formica table.

Mr Untidy continued, 'Mr Mulheron, we believe you have been working for at least four months. Pending an investigation and a further meeting, your benefits are suspended. This process may take some time to complete. Any subsequent benefits due to you will be minus the sum owed to the state for that four-month period. We will, of course, allow this to be repaid over a longer period of time, should you wish that to be the case. You do have the option to cease claiming benefit and continuing in your current paid employment.'

'How very fucking kind of you.' Still seated, Peter arched across the table, his large intimidating frame leading the colleagues to lean slowly back in their chairs. 'Ye know, I've worked longer than you've probably been alive, ya wee prick. I'll keep the small bit of dignity that you lot can't take off me, and bid you fuckers goodbye. Send me a letter telling me what you're doing.' He rose swiftly and turned to leave the room.

'There is another option.' The diminutive woman finally spoke in a soft voice.

'Sit down, Peter. My name is Detective Chief Inspector Henshaw.'

Peter looked on incredulously as the staff door closed; clearly Mr Untidy was not required at this stage.

She quickly flashed her warrant card, just long enough for Peter to catch the words *Serious Crime Squad*. She glanced at the chair, her eyes taking control. Peter followed her instruction, while continuing to maintain eye contact.

'We've been watching your employer for the last eighteen months. We believe – we *know* – Eddie Quinn is *the* major player in the procurement and distribution of Class A drugs in Paisley and beyond. Probably feeding the whole of the west of Scotland.' Clasping her hands, it was now her turn to lean across the desk. 'We want to put him away for a long time, but we need help.'

Peter folded his arms across his chest and laughed nervously. 'Eh? Naw, naw, no way. Are ye serious? Touting? That's a death wish around here. Anyway, I know fuck all. Seriously, are you mental? No thanks, detective I'll take the hit from that other mob and my weans might starve, but at least we'll have all our limbs.'

'Peter, I don't think you understand. The way I see it, you have just been done by the social, bang to rights. If you don't go back to work for Quinn just as we are about to turn him over, who do you think his first suspicions will fall on? Yes, you. And if they don't, we'll make sure it somehow makes its way into the court papers to steer his henchmen in your direction.'

'You bitch! What the fuck did I do to deserve this?'

'Nothing. Wrong place, wrong time. You seem like a decent bloke, a family man, just trying to get by, and you're somebody we think we can trust.' She lowered her voice to garner his support. 'Look, we're nearly there. We just need eyes and ears in the taxi office to pick up any additional intel, just small snippets, conversations about where the deliveries are going. If you help me out, I'll sort things this end with the social and make sure no one suspects you.'

'I'm off.' Peter rose again to leave.

'I'll need an answer within the next twenty-four hours. Here's my card. Call me direct,' she said confidently, her bleached-blonde hair falling over her sharp features. 'Bye.'

He slammed the door shut and the partition walls reverberated. 'This is fucking nonsense. I don't know anything, honestly.' He pleaded for sympathy as he retook his seat.

'Look, Peter, we know you don't like what he does. We're aware you had an argument about the smack deliveries. We just need a little bit more to shut his operation down for good. However, we want the whole distribution network, from where it's coming in from to the two-bit dealers in the schemes. All I'm asking is that you spend a bit of time round the office and get back on the main run. I'll check in with you every now and then for anything you may have picked up. That okay?'

'And you'll sort out this lot?' Peter tossed his head towards the door.

'Yes, no problem,' Henshaw asserted.

'I want you to help my boy, Michael, get an apprenticeship somewhere, anywhere out of Paisley. You must have contacts in the Merchant Navy or with a contractor somewhere. No British Army. If that's not agreed, yer getting fuck all.'

'After the info you provide is verified I'll sort it, guaranteed. You will still receive a letter advising that your benefits are suspended pending investigation but just ignore that, moan about it. We don't know how far Quinn's network stretches, so everything is very tight. I'll be in touch. Nevertheless – anything at all, call me. Oh, and slam the door on the way out.'

Chapter Thirteen

THE WHITE LIGHTING BOUNCED off the polished pine furniture as Cal took his seat in Court Number 2. His opposite number from the procurator fiscal was already in place, busily highlighting sentences in the witness statements piled up on his desk.

'Morning, Mr Lynch. Joining me for a fun-filled day, I see,' he smirked, raising his unkempt, wiry, eyebrows above his large round glasses. 'Your client has amassed quite a record.'

'Well, I'm thankful that the law doesn't allow that information to be revealed to our lovely jury, John,' Cal responded curtly, setting out his files on the desk.

'Only pulling your leg, child. I've been in here for nigh on thirty years and couldn't really give a shit about your client, or any of the others that cross my path. My mind is already on Friday and the flight to lovely Tuscany and the several bottles of red that await my presence. So please, don't let this run over. I hear you made quite a reputation for yourself round the circuit in London?' His bloated, red nose clearly showed a liking for wine and his attitude, coupled with his ageing appearance, gave the impression of someone biding his time until retirement.

Cal knew his task was challenging. John Burns was a formidable prosecutor fiscal who had a high success rate; he was frequently sought by Strathclyde Police as their preferred choice to lead on similar cases.

Franny McGurn entered the court from the holding cells flanked by two police officers. He was well-presented in a smart dark-blue suit and light-blue tie. Cal advised him at their pre-meeting to keep his hands below the screen in the dock; the Indian ink tattoos of *love, hate* and *fuck the polis* might have a detrimental effect on the jury's opinion of the accused.

Cal nodded towards his client but received no reaction. Franny McGurn was now in court mode. This only required him to set his blue eyes on the sheriff throughout the trial, no glancing at witnesses, lawyers and, importantly, the jury. Don't allow any preconceived thoughts of a guilty verdict to be reinforced by an unfortunate glance at a nervous jury member.

McGurn had been a continuous visitor to the building for most his adult life and had a charge sheet as long as his thick, muscular arm. A product of a dysfunctional family, he had learned to defend and fend for himself as a teenager and latterly as an enforcer with the local crime clan. Quinn had witnessed his abilities as he faced up to older rivals who sought to encroach on the embryonic local drug market. After that performance, he had joined the payroll and lived at Quinn's palatial home. He would run through a brick wall for his master; he had sought to prove himself a loyal servant from the outset and always carried out instructions without deliberation.

Cal listened attentively as the clerk read the trial diet then he addressed the bench. 'Not guilty, Your Honour.'

He slipped into daydream mode as the clerk balloted the jury, read the indictment, and administered the oath for those selected.

Sheriff George Dunlop outlined the procedure to the sworn-in jury. Although he seemed to have permanent frown lines, he was an affable man and tried hard to relax the jurors with jokes – though he often failed to garner a response from the nervous incumbents.

Dunlop had worked the bench for some fifteen years. A failed Conservative candidate at the election two years earlier, he had stood on a local manifesto to clean up the growing drug epidemic engulfing Paisley. The people spoke during the democratic process; he scraped just enough votes to retain his deposit.

Although the sheriff's primary role was to ensure the processes of justice were followed and the jury advised where appropriate, Dunlop's background put Cal on edge. No doubt the sheriff would seek to influence the jury in such clear-cut cases as the one about to play out in his court.

'*Francis McGurn, 12 Spencer Avenue. You are indicted at the instance of Her Majesty's Advocate and the charge against you is that on 2nd June in Wellmeadow public toilets, Paisley, while acting alone, you did assault Ian Saddler, strike him with a knife or similar instrument, punch him on the head and knock him to the ground, all to his severe injury and disfigurement.*'

John Burns called the first witness for the prosecution: Ian Saddler. A middle-aged man shuffled slowly across the room to the witness box, his head down. He looked decidedly older than his years as a court assistant assisted him to the box.

'Are you able to stand, Mr Saddler, or would you require a seat?' enquired the sheriff.

Saddler waved his hand dismissively. His face was still raw with scar tissue from the left side of his small forehead to below his chin. Cal knew what to expect next from the jury: a quick study of the horrific injuries followed by a stare at the accused. Could McGurn have done this to this poor, frail man?

McGurn sat impassively, his compact features devoid of movement or emotion. His large shaved cranium gave the impression that it was designed for head butting, which was something he was proficient in delivering.

John Burns tugged on his faded black gown as he stood up. 'Mr

Saddler, please relax as much as you possibly can. If we can go back to the second of June of this year. Can you recall the events of that night?'

'I can. I had just locked up my new shop and wen ... went to the public toilets before heading for the bus home.' Saddler's eyes darted around the room. 'I just got to the urinal when I felt a huge pain on the left side of my head. I fell to the ground and landed on my back'. Closing his eyes tightly, he gripped the edge of the witness box. 'I looked up and saw a frightening, hate-filled face hanging over me. He grabbed me by the coat and started pounding me with his fist. After that, I can't remember a thing.'

'Can I take you back further, Mr Saddler? Have you ever been approached to pay a type fee or protection money?'

'When I took the shop on, two young guys in cheap suits called in and said there would be an uplift on the property every week. I chased them out the door.'

'For the benefit of members of the jury, Mr Saddler, could you tell the court the injuries you received from the savage attack you suffered?'

'I have... I have not worked since. A broken jaw, fractured eye socket, dizzy spells, twenty-eight stitches along this cheek. All because I wouldn't pay protection money.'

'And, Mr Saddler, can you point out the person within this court who you picked out at a subsequent identity parade, and who you believe is responsible for this vicious attack?'

Mr Saddler, his laboured breathing heard throughout the silent courtroom, raised a shaking finger directly at McGurn, who never flinched.

'Thank you, Mr Saddler. I also refer the jury to item reference 1.1 within the evidence documents provided – details of Mr Saddler's positive identification of the accused at an identity parade which took place at Mill Street Police station. It should be noted that this procedure was two months after the assault, due to the fact that Mr Saddler was hospitalised and unable to see with clear vision a full *seven* weeks from the night in question.' The prosecutor took his seat, satisfied that the die had been cast with the first witness.

Cal rose slightly from his chair. 'No questions, Your Honour.' He glanced towards the public benches to see Quinn's other henchman, Nails, glaring.

Joyce was sitting behind him, head buried in a file. They had been in the office right up to the early hours, running over the witness' statements and case files. This was not part of the plan.

John Burns' next witness was already in the box as Cal raised his head from his notes. 'Mr Dawson, can you take the court through the events you witnessed in the public toilets on the evening of the second of June this year,' the prosecutor asked.

Dawson turned his bony face, revealing a heavily tattooed neck, and glanced over to the public benches where he met the eye of what was clearly a CID officer present to witness that proceedings went the way they expected. 'Well, I was burstin' on the way home 'n' nipped doon for a pish, 'n' that's when it happened.'

'Take a wee step back, Mr Dawson. Was there anyone present in the toilets when you entered?'

'Aye, there was an auld boy and him ooer there, they were at the urinals. Ah stood in between them tae dae a piss, then that guy pushed past me 'n' leathered the auld guy. Ah got a fright and jumped back. Ah didnae want ma new bleached jeans splattered with blood.'

'Did you try to intervene and stop the assault?'

'Naw, he was well scary. He looked up at me 'n' told me tae fuck off oot. Sorry fur swearing.'

'And you are convinced that the man on trial here is the same individual you witnessed carry out an attack on a defenceless man. He is also the person you subsequently selected from an identification parade at Mill Street Police Station?'

'Aw aye, definitely him.' Dawson was growing in confidence, pleased to be doing his civic duty; he raised his thumb tellingly towards the police officer in the gallery.

'No further questions.'

Cal rose and walked slowly to the lectern. 'Mr Dawson, my name is Cal Lynch. Tell me, do you frequent Paisley on a regular basis.'

'Naw, Ah usually just stay in ma scheme in Johnstone, but that day oor chemist was closed 'n' Ah haud tae find wan in the toon tae get ma script. So Ah jumped oan a bus tae the West End.'

'Can I ask what medication you are prescribed, Mr Dawson?'

'Valium.'

'Do you take any other medication, Mr Dawson?'

'All sorts. Ah used tae be oan the smack but Ah'm clean noo. The Valium keeps me calm and helps me sleep. Ah've been aff the gear for nearly a year, so well proud.' He smiled, straightening his back and puffing out his shallow chest, his happy grin revealing a mouthful of black teeth.

It was now Cal's turn to glance towards the plain-clothes cop. He had this figured out as he circled passages of the witness statement with his red pen. 'Mr Dawson, can you recall the last time you visited the public toilets on Wellmeadow St?'

'That wis ma first time.'

'Your first time? Let's be clear, you haven't visited these premises previously?' Cal glanced at the witness then met the eye of several of the jury, ensuring they were paying attention.

'Naw.' Dawson looked at him, confused.

'And you were only at the urinals within the facility. Is that correct?'

'Aye, the urinals that's right,' Dawson replied, nodding assertively.

'No further questions. Thank you for your cooperation Mr Dawson.' Cal took his chair, writing quickly on his notepad while his opposite number scanned his notes. The older lawyer knew something was not quite right; he just had to figure out what.

'Mr Burns, your next witness?' Sheriff Dunlop pressed the prosecutor impatiently, tapping his pen on the elevated bench.

DS Lawrie stood on the witness stand, police notebook in hand, straight back, his unshaven chin held high. An experienced officer, the surroundings wouldn't faze him; no doubt he would be methodical and disciplined, with nothing left to chance.

'Detective Sergeant Lawrie, you were the first officer on scene and consequently the lead investigating officer in relation to this alleged assault – is that correct?' Burns asked, peering over his glasses.

'Correct, sir.'

'Can you run through the sequence of events in relation to the second of June, please?' Burns returned to his seat and recommenced scouring his case notes.

Lawrie slowly flicked through his small black notebook. 'I received a radio call at approximately 18:00hrs to attend the Wellmeadow public toilet, where an individual had been assaulted. On entering the premises, I found a middle-aged male, who I later identified as Mr Ian Saddler, semi-conscious. From my immediate examination,' Lawrie paused to look at the jury, 'I noted that the individual had lacerations to his head and a severely swollen eye. I immediately checked and found a weak pulse. I radioed for an ambulance and uniformed support to secure the crime scene and the evidence.'

'Was there anyone else present, detective?' Burns enquired.

'No, sir.'

'Let's move on. As the senior investigating officer on this case, can you outline to the court how you apprehended the accused?' Burns asked, leaning on the lectern.

'Our investigations indicated that the person of interest had gone to ground and was planning to hide out in London until such time as things quietened down. He was arrested on Platform 1 at Glasgow Central, while boarding a London bound train on the fourth of June at 07:00 hrs.' Again Lawrie glanced assuredly at the jury. 'No further evidence was captured during the interview process. Forensic evidence from the scene, and two witness statements linking the accused to the crime and his subsequent identification, led to the charges as outlined.'

Burns returned to his seat and Cal quickly went to the lectern. Then, stepping back, he began to walk around the front of the court, hands in pockets. He oozed confidence. 'DS Lawrie, you were the first responder to the incident?'

'That's correct, sir,' Lawrie responded.

'Does an officer of your senior rank usually respond to such calls?' Cal asked, turning on his heels.

'Mr Lynch, this is not an American movie set. Use the lectern or stay seated. Understood?' The Sheriff glared at Cal, clearly unhappy that his court could be turned into a sideshow.

'When the call comes in we have a duty to respond – no matter your rank ... sir.' Lawrie smiled.

Cal flicked through his file and lifted a paper from the lectern. 'So, did you respond to the other – let me see – twelve 999 calls that were received and logged within K Division that evening?'

'If I'd been available, of course I would have, sir.'

'And your ten-hour shift the previous day? Eight 999 calls, three of which were serious assaults. Any of those?' Cal stared intently as Lawrie glowered.

'Again sir. If available, without doubt I would have. That's my job, sir.' He was agitated with the line of questioning and expected the fiscal to intervene on his behalf. Cal's questioning, which bore little relevance to the crime, irked him. Lawrie's jaw tightened and his glare became more evident.

'You state that Mr Saddler was alone when you entered the scene of the assault. Can you advise how the witness, Mr Dawson, was located?'

Lawrie welcomed the change in tack and read from his notes. 'Mr David Dawson presented himself at Mill Street Station and volunteered a statement.'

'Detective, as the witness advised in his evidence to this court, he is a recovering heroin addict. In all your years of experience serving the good people of Paisley, is it common for such individuals to actively engage with the police in such a manner?'

Lawrie understood Cal's intention to discredit the main witness in front of the jury and sow doubt that the events had not actually taken place as the police had presented them.

Lawrie had won many cases from the witness box and, yes, he had bent the rules at times to put individuals away. David Dawson had owed him a turn. He had called in at Mill Street the day after the assault to answer an outstanding warrant. Their conversation had led to a statement that embellished the truth slightly as to what he'd witnessed at Wellmeadow.

'Not in my experience, but Mr Dawson was clearly traumatised and still in shock from the vicious attack he had witnessed on a defenceless man. I'm sure anyone who was exposed to such violence would do their utmost to ensure it didn't happen again to someone else ... sir.'

'Hmm. Thank you, DS Lawrie. No further questions from me.'

'Detective Sergeant Lawrie, were you able to establish a motive for this attack during the course of your investigations?' Burns asked quickly, trying to return the narrative to the victim.

'The victim was quite insistent that he was being pressured to pay protection money to a security organisation for new premises he had taken on. This organisation is well known to the police. We have, as yet, been unable to confirm or establish the link to which the victim refers.'

'No further witnesses from the fiscal, Your Honour.' John Burns sat down, satisfied to have sown the seed of a motive.

'Mr Lynch, your turn,' Sheriff Dunlop advised, his head darting between his notes and the jury.

'Defence calls Mr Robert Newton, Your Honour.'

Robert Newton filled the witness stand with his heavy frame. Sweat was already gathering, staining his neatly ironed, council-branded T-shirt.

'Mr Newton, could you explain your role with the local council, please?' Cal asked. He remained in his seat; he liked to change tack with witnesses. It allowed the jury to recall various stages in the trial process. If he followed a repetitive routine, all the events and evidence may just roll into one and key points were lost.

'Aye, I'm in charge of aw the maintenance of the council's public toilets and another coupla buildings,' Newton replied proudly, wiping his forehead and neck with a discoloured handkerchief.

'And the public toilet at Wellmeadow, according to the maintenance log submitted to the court, was upgraded and repainted on the first of June – the day before the alleged incident. Is that correct?'

'Aye, repainted all the walls and new pipes added to remove the auld corroded works. It just opened late morning of the second, then we had tae close it again … obviously.' The witness laughed uncomfortably.

Cal looked across the desk at his opposite number. 'So just to clarify, Mr Newton, the walls were repainted the day previously and the facility was only opened a matter of hours before the alleged assault at approximately 6pm?'

'Correct. Two coats of magnolia. Place wis lookin' like a new pin.'

'Thank you, Mr Newton, no more questions.'

The fiscal was scouring Newton's statement and log sheets. 'No questions, Your Honour.' His complexion was growing redder by the minute.

'Your final witness, I believe, Mr Lynch. We will all be home by lunch at this rate.' Dunlop laughed towards the jury and received a lukewarm response.

'Can you please provide your name and job title for the jury?' Cal was back on his feet facing the witness box.

'Stuart Sutherland, Scene of Crime Officer, Strathclyde Police.' The middle-aged man stood no more than five foot tall, with glasses perched on his shiny bald head. His protruding stomach marred the look of his smart, three-piece tweed suit.

'Mr Sutherland, can you inform the jury of your role in gathering evidence at the scene of the alleged assault at the Wellmeadow Public Toilets on the second of June this year?'

Sutherland lowered his glasses over his soft brown eyes to read from his notebook. 'I was the forensic officer in charge of the locus. I gathered samples from the scene, noted in the incident log all those who entered the premises after the assault, and those we knew were present at the time of the incident, of course.'

'Could you elaborate, please? What type of samples did you collect?' Cal asked, quietly.

Mr Sutherland flicked through the pages quickly, closed the book and replied, 'Blood samples, skin samples, hair, footprints, multiple fingerprints and a full palm print.'

'A full palm print? Can I draw you and the jury's attention to page fifteen in the witness pack, referenced as forensic item 3745. May I add this was not included in the Prosecutor Fiscal evidence bundle. Can you confirm Mr Sutherland who the full palm print belongs to?' Cal held up the page for emphasis and ensured the clerk of the court was on hand to point out the page to the jury members.

The forensic officer double-checked item 3745 and spoke confidently. 'Our follow-up processes show there was sufficient ridge detail to identify print marks. This subsequently allowed a comparison to be made from those provided by witnesses who'd been present at the scene, or stated at a later date to be at the scene. This was followed up by submission to the Ident1 database which also matched the print to that of a Mr David Dawson.'

Cal now took his voice up an octave to accentuate the importance of what was being revealed. 'Mr Sutherland, from the layout on the drawing of the toilets in front of you, page thirty of the witness pack, reference 4600, where was this print recovered?'

'This print was recovered from the first cubicle toilet within the premises.' The officer pointed at a large map.

'Let us be clear – not at the urinals but in the cubicle?' Cal enquired.

'Yes, the cubicle, it was sited on the wall above the toilet,' Sutherland stated, insistently.

'And how, in your professional opinion, was the palm print left on the wall, Mr Sutherland?' Cal probed, leading the witness to where he knew exposed the weakness in the prosecution case.

'I believe the individual was leaning his hand *against* the wall while urinating into the toilet.'

'Are you positive? How certain are you regarding the location and positioning of the print? Could you be mistaken?' Cal was asking questions that might be going through the jury members' heads, as well as gently stirring the expert witness.

Mr Sutherland turned to look at the sheriff for guidance, the bright lights bouncing off his polished dome. He received no response. 'I've been twenty-five years in the forensic business, man and boy. I don't make mistakes. A full palm print can only be identified, in such a location, in the circumstances I have described. In addition, everything is checked and peer checked before we leave a scene, similarly when we review back at the lab,' he responded, contemptuously.

'So, help me then, please, Mr Sutherland. The previous day the toilets had been painted with two coats of magnolia, and only opened hours before the alleged assault.' Cal faced the jury then swiftly turned to eye the forensics' man. 'A witness to that incident, a Mr David Dawson, stated – and I quote – *"he visited the toilets for the first time and was situated at the middle urinal when the assault took place."* Unquote. He then left quickly and *thankfully* did his civic duty and presented himself at Mill Street Police Station to give a full and detailed account of what took place. How could he possibly have left a full palm print in the newly painted cubicle?'

Mr Sutherland turned slightly to face the jury, feeling his professionalism and credibility were being called into question. 'I can't answer for the statement to which you refer. I'm presenting the forensic facts collected at the scene by my office. Facts, Mr Lynch, with evidence collated against best practice.'

That's the answer and precise attitude I wanted you to show, Cal thought.

'The forensic facts? I could not put it better myself. Thank you, Mr Sutherland. No more questions, Your Honour.'

John Burns was already making eye contact with the plain-clothed officer sitting at the rear of the court. He rose slowly, his face gradually moving from crimson to deep red. 'Your Honour, the Crown will not be presenting any further evidence and will no longer be pursuing this case.'

'Yes!' McGurn slammed his fist on the side of the dock, startling the court.

The sheriff stared at him for what seemed to be an eternity, then he spoke. 'Members of the jury, I would like to express my gratitude for your contribution today. I have no doubt you have found some of the evidence harrowing. As you have heard, the prosecution no longer wishes to proceed with this indictment so you are dismissed from further service this week. Mr McGurn, you have clearly also heard the procurator fiscal. You are free to leave the court.'

Cal collected his papers and glanced at the public bench as Quinn gave a crooked smile and quietly sneaked out of the court.

'You were right, boss. They left a hole and we found it.' Joyce beamed in delight and slapped Cal on the back.

'Looks like I'll make France after all. See you again, Mr Lynch,' John Burns whispered as he waddled towards the exit

Cal shook McGurn's hand as he left the dock. No words were shared. Exposing the flaws in the case had all seemed rather easy. He would put that to the back of his mind for now.

'The boss is having a celebratory drink back at the office. He will see you there.' Nails didn't wait for a response as he walked quickly from the court.

* * *

Cal woke fresh from the previous late-night celebrations. He had ensured he stayed sober, only sipping on the one malt throughout the evening though Joyce had become gluttonous with the free bar. The party had gone on until the small hours, with Quinn holding centre stage and his employees hanging on every word.

'Let me show you some of our achievements Cal,' he'd announced guiding him towards the framed pictures on the silk-covered wall. 'We never get recognition. Dialysis machines, baby incubators, training schemes, minibuses to take pensioners, kids and football teams abroad on holidays they could only dream about otherwise. And we're crooks? Harassment, that's what it is, plain and simple.'

Quinn wandered back to his desk, picked up a tattered, leather bound book and handed it to Cal. '*Delinquent Man* by Cesare Lombroso.'

'Ah, yes. His study into the Favara Brotherhood in Sicily, believed to be the first Cosa Nostra. A very interesting read,' Cal asserted, content that his familiarity with the subject would allow the conversation to flow.

'Exactly, I read it at least once a year. And the reason it sits permanently on my desk? Because Lombroso states that certain deformities indicate criminals – criminal stigmata. And young guys like McGurn, with his tattoos and aggressive expression, is the modern day equivalent. I'm the modern equivalent too because I'm successful. New money - where did he get it? Must be a criminal.'

Quinn was loosening up, thought Cal, must be the brandy. 'An interesting analogy, Mr Quinn, but if innocent you have nothing to worry about.' He raised his eyebrows.

'In this town if you have a good lawyer you've nothing to worry about,' Quinn said. 'Here, more whisky.'

* * *

'So tell me, Lawrie, why was yesterday so simple? You went to court with a flawed case against McGurn, which a junior counsel could have seen through, and folded it at the first opportunity.'

'Christ, I'd thought you'd be happy, Cal. You won the case, didn't you? And we do know he's ruined that poor man's life.'

Lawrie lit another cigarette and blew smoke out his wide nostrils. He has spent his whole police career in Paisley, rejecting the opportunity of further promotion elsewhere within the force. Having lost his only sister to a drug overdose Lawrie was determined, and obsessive, in his pursuit of smashing the local the dealers and the networks which supplied them. He had been radioed to attend a report of two bodies lying in a dilapidated lane. To find and cradle his sister, who had left the family home months before after a row about her drug use, was unbearable. At times his methods were outside the recognised rule book but the image of his beautiful sister, her body decimated beyond recognition with a bloodied needle hanging from her track marked arm, never left him.

'Look, there's bigger sharks circling Quinn. The details haven't been shared, but we were told to throw this up with enough for the fiscal to proceed. Expose Quinn as a gangster again to get the local and national press to start digging then, when *others* move in, it'll be easier to bring him down. Folk will be keener to provide info. Anyway, it gets you further embedded with him. He'll be more relaxed around you. You never know, they may drop some wee bits of info.'

Cal lowered the window and sniffed his cashmere coat. 'Could we maybe meet somewhere with a bit of fresh air next time?'

'I've still not fully sussed you out, but I don't think yer one of his lackeys – yet. Anything for me? You partied until the small hours – must have been some interesting conversations?'

'God, I don't believe it. So simple,' Cal whispered, under his breath.

'What is?' Lawrie sat up attentively. 'This is about distribution? We know his empire is built on it, we just cannae nail him.'

Cal looked directly at Lawrie; he still didn't entirely trust him. The lines on the seasoned detective's forehead tightened as he awaited a response. 'Oh, nothing,' he said. 'I was just thinking out loud. Let me come back to you if I get anything.'

I'll feed Lawrie small snippets to test if he is on Quinn's payroll, Cal thought. *Then I'll reveal how the empire functions. Another step to bring him down.*

Chapter Fourteen

'BOYS, GATHER ROUND PLEASE.' Father MacDonald ushered the altar servers into the sacristy. 'Right, boys. Tonight's Mass is a very special event for your parish and for me, your priest. My boss, Bishop Hassan, will be the main celebrant so be on your best behaviour.' His head darted between the attendees, gauging their reaction. 'Remind me who was on the bells at early Sunday Mass last week? Young Taggart, was it you?'

Taggart hid behind his fellow servers and lowered his head as he recalled his exuberance.

'You're not auditioning for *Trumpton*, sonny. Short burst, understand? And Delaney,' the priest continued, dropping his face to the boy's ear, his shiny red complexion growing darker by the second. 'If I ever catch you and that Keenan drinking the altar wine again, you'll not be dismissed from serving but will be on Stations of the Cross for the next six months. Now get your albs on, his Holiness will be here shortly.'

He placed the green chasuble over the white alb and stole that swathed his rotund body. 'You never know, I might get a quiet Parish out of this,' he murmured to himself.

Father Dan MacDonald had arrived at St Mary's Parish in Paisley from Scotus College, Rome, eight years earlier. Privately educated and sheltered from harsh urban realities while being raised in an affluent area of Gourock, he struggled with the daily challenges his parishioners faced. Frustrated by his own lack of empathy, he felt he was failing in his calling. His tough exterior and gruff attitude allowed him to maintain a safe, emotional, distance from his parishioners; his flock's devotion to the faith was inspiring, though their needs were more than spiritual.

'It's mobbed oot there,' Delaney announced, sounding surprised. 'We getting a bung for the night?' he enquired, to no one in particular while sniffing the lid of the decanted wine.

'Doubt it, mate. I've only had weigh-ins at weddings and christenings. There's cake in the hall after – that'll do,' replied Taggart, while emptying the incense boat into the thurible.

Sarah read over her bidding prayer for the tenth time within the last two minutes.

'Don't be nervous. Just do as we practised – count to three in between paragraphs. I'm up first, then you. We'll be fine, trust me,' Liz reassured her partner.

'It's really busy. I wasn't expecting this busy.' Sarah looked over her shoulder, scanning the large chapel and finding Liz's dad in the crowd.

'We'll be done in no time. There's two before us. After that, the new girl is singing. That should be a laugh.'

The congregation stood to greet the procession led by the three altar boys, all wearing ill-fitting robes, and the parish priest. The tall, authoritative figure of Bishop Hassan, carrying his ceremonial crosier, smiled affably to the parishioners as he made his way towards the gothic altar designed by the great Cuthbert Pugin almost one hundred years ago. The nave filled with the rich smell of incense as Taggart swung the thurible incessantly. The bishop would use it in a ritual gesture of honour around the altar.

Peter had nearly switched off already. His mind was racing, going over and over his steps. He was merely on nodding terms with God and his attendance this evening was linked to trying to get a minute with Dixie, a regular Mass goer, to run through his predicament. However, Dixie's no-show meant he was no doubt sipping Guinness in his other favourite Vatican.

Peter had gone back on the main taxi run without much discussion. He noted drop offs, the constant movement of packages, who was involved but didn't seem to touch anything. The wannabe gangsters were only too happy to get their hands dirty to obtain street cred. Interestingly, there were irregular visits to the office from an individual who dropped off keys, spoke to no one, disappeared, and returned within a couple of hours of arrival.

Peter always contacted the cop handler from a phone box at Paisley Cross and passed on what he had learned using some of the descriptive techniques they'd taught him to recall information.

* * *

I wandered then away from town to a quiet lonely place.
I found a clear unruffled pool and I gazed upon my face.
And I saw the colour of me more clearly than if I had never
been blind.
The lines of envy around the lips and the greed and the hate
in the eye.
And I turned away, yes I turned away.

The congregation fell silent and awaited the greeting as the opening hymn ended.

'Brothers and Sisters we are gathered here today as one to celebrate the talents of our young people, all of our young people. I sincerely hope you enjoy and participate in our Holy Mass as we look to strengthen our community bonds.' The bishop's voice echoed through the large expanse aided by the recent addition of microphones.

'Is that the bishop? Very softly spoken, lovely eyes,' Suzie whispered to Cal.

'You want to defrock him? New bishop, quite left wing, I hear. Surprise appointment.'

'You're full of loads of useless info, aren't you, Ironside. You're such a bore, researching everything,' she teased, clutching his hand and moving closer in the pew.

'We're nearly there. Just his sermon then the weans' bidding prayers and we are home and dry,' Peter whispered to Mikey.

'Wait till ye hear Mairi-Clare sing, Da. Voice of an angel.'

'Smitten again, son, I see.'

The bishop stood at the ornate marble altar, the polished brass railings in front of him reflecting the bright lights hanging from the large archways. An imposing crucifixion, hanging from the ceiling, dominated the chapel and drew everyone's attention as they entered. The bidding prayer readers sat nervously waiting for their cue, going over their readings and songs.

'Children, parents, teachers, friends. May I thank you again for joining us in this celebration of talents. Father Dan has told me so much about the strong community which exists here in your parish and throughout the West End of Paisley.' The bishop's voice reached every corner of the large chapel.

Have I? thought the local priest.

'A community that continues to thrive and support each other, despite the negative outside influences and pressures which challenge and seek to destroy it. So what are these challenges?'

'I've got him down for 30 minutes what about you?' Cal murmured.

'Don't be rude, Cal. This sounds interesting.' Suzie nipped his arm in disapproval.

'We are in an age where consumerism and individualism seek to dominate our society,' the bishop continued. 'Where the family values, which promote strong, sustainable community life, are viewed as old hat or from a redundant era that will no longer satisfy our insatiable materialistic needs.'

He moved away from the altar towards the congregation, engaging them as he spoke, his hand resting on the shoulders of a young child who was sitting rigid in her school uniform at the end of a pew.

'We are in an age where the government of the day can extinguish the future of our young people, their hopes, dreams and aspirations with the stroke of a pen as they continue to pursue this scorched-earth policy of de-industrialisation. Decimating our communities, *this* community. Children, young people lost to a world of despair and, in some cases, the scourge of drugs perpetrated by the evil amongst us.' Lowering his head, he continued with his impassioned sermon.

'I call on and pray that this government does not forget the talented young people we are about to hear from in this parish and town but provides hope. I call on and pray for my fellow priests to take up our Lord's mantle and speak out where there is injustice, raise issues with local and national officials who are risking the very fabric of our society. Also I call on you, our exceptionally gifted young people, to have confidence in your talents and strengths and may the enduring love of Jesus our saviour guide you on the journey through life. Please let us hear the bidding prayers and hymns of our young people.'

'Don't think he'll be getting a red hat if he keeps going on like that,' Suzie whispered in Cal's ear.

'Who knew Mass could trigger a revolution, Suzie? Good on him. I might come back if this is the usual standard,' Cal responded, in an equally lowered tone.

Mary stood with her small tambourine in hand, staring out at the congregation. She caught the glance of her mother who was beaming with pride as her daughter stood on the altar steps. This was Mary's first time inside the chapel since her dad's remains were received and sat before the altar. She'd been adamant that she would never darken its door again, or pray to an invisible being that had taken her dad, her best friend. She had railed against the church, so her mum was surprised when Mary had committed to taking part. *That girl Mairi-Clare is a good influence,* she thought. *I hope they stay friends.*

'Lord graciously hear us.'

Sarah could barely hear the subdued parishioners' response to the bidding prayers as it was competing with her heartbeat that was getting louder by the second.

'Two minutes and we are done,' Liz said. 'Just two minutes.'

'Dear Lord.'

One, two, three.

'We pray for our families here today. May they continue to shine in this ever-changing world. We pray for our parents as they seek to provide and nurture us, their children.'

One, two, three.

'Lord hear us.'

'Lord graciously hear us.'

Well done, Liz. Now my turn, thought Sarah, as she stood on the box that elevated her towards the mic, her small frame disappearing behind the polished marble Ambo. She looked out at what seemed like thousands of eyes staring directly at her. She scanned the audience for a friendly face and settled on Peter, who seemed a million, sad, miles away. The happy, cheery man she'd met just two months earlier and had got to know on her visits was long since gone. Liz had said she was worried about her dad – all he wanted was to work, but that woman had decided that his type of contribution was not required any more. He was of no value, cast-off, as if he were nothing.

'Dear Lord.'

One, two, three.

'Maggie Thatcher.' Her voice seemed to grow with each syllable.

One, two, three.

'FUCK HER.'

All the eyes, which were now focused and fixated on her, seemed to double in size as she completed her 'prayer'. Okay, she'd altered it slightly from the sheet in front of her, but Peter needed this prayer – he needed a job.

One, two, three.

'Lord hear us.'

The thousand eyes now left Sarah and fixed their gaze on Bishop Hasson. The bishop nodded.

'Lord graciously hear us,' they responded loudly in unison.

'We're on, Mary.'

Mary stared vacantly into the nave of the church, her eyes resting on a woman with sharp features and long, glossy black hair that cascaded over her shoulders and framed her pale complexion. *Overdressed in a red camel coat*, she thought. Dangling, diamond earrings glistened and darted in the bright white light, high above her. *That's classy, but not for here – not this place.*

'Wait here,' Mairi-Clare swung her guitar over her shoulder and, with a couple of steps, was at the bishop's side.

Father Dan closed his eyes. What more could go wrong? He was sweating incessantly, his permanent flushed skin turning to beetroot.

Mairi-Clare spoke quietly to the bishop who smiled in response. Then she said, 'Right, Mary, change of plan.'

'Our young people will continue to showcase their talents not with the song you have in your missal but a moving piece that speaks of enduring love,' the bishop announced confidently.

'Mary, listen to me.' Mairi-Clare looked into her friend's eyes. 'I've heard you sing. You have to also let these people hear you. We need to show we are all normal, remember. I know what happened to your dad and that you hate this place, but he loved singing and he loved you.'

'No.' Mary's body was beginning to stiffen.

'I'm going to play the guitar. You turn and face them. Just pick a spot and get lost in your singing. We are singing *Bright Blue Rose*. I know your dad loved to hear you sing that.'

Mary's face and body tightened in fear, her eyes staring at the white marble steps on which she stood. Her dad had taught her the song, verse by verse. His friend back home in Cork, Jimmy McCarthy, had written it.

'One day it'll be a hit,' he would say. 'Jimmy will be famous, Ah'm tellin ye.'

Gradually she glimpsed at where her dad's remains had been

placed and her mind eased as she remembered their good times. Her mood quickly changed as she recalled the last time she'd seen him. Skipping down to his garage to deliver his lunch on Saturday mornings was always something she looked forward to. The garage would be quiet and he would let her play on the empty buses, sit in the driving cab and watch him work through the large clean windscreen. They would share lunch, sing and laugh his half-hour break away.

That day was different. The rusted garage doors were half closed and the pavement taped off as a stern police officer struggled to hold back an inquisitive crowd. She remembered squeezing to the front as a stretcher was carried to a waiting ambulance with a large body covered by a white, blood-stained blanket.

'Guy didnae stand a chance. Ah heard the hydraulic jack collapsed, crushed him tae death under the front a' the bus. Poor bastard,' whispered a worker from a nearby yard, loud enough for Mary to hear.

Suddenly a lifeless arm slipped from the edge of the stretcher and she let out a piercing scream. The hand bore her father's silver wedding ring. Her mind had blocked out what happened next; she could only recall waking on the living-room couch, her mother crying ceaselessly in the corner.

Mary did not dare look at her mum. She glanced at the diamond-wearing, long-haired model type then sharply at the large clock at the rear of the church. Dad said the clock was for the priest to decide how long he was going to waffle on during his sermons – 'if he's in a bad mood pet, we're here for a while.'

Back to staring at the model.

Right, Dad, this is for you. I miss you every day but maybe this will help me start again. Mum thinks I'm grumpy because I'm still grieving. It's not that. I'm raging because I can't remember the sound of your voice – the voice that laughed as you shook the branches of the cherry tree and covered me in scented pink petals, the voice that read to me and recited Irish lullabies with that distinct lilt. Her tears began to fall from her chin onto her patent shoes, dulling the black shine with each direct hit. *I only hear your voice when I sing.*

'Okay,' she nodded nervously to her partner.

The distinct sound of the guitar seemed to become more pronounced, accentuated, allowing Mary to tune her inner ear.

I skim-med across black water
Without once submerging
Onto the banks of an urban morning
That hungers the first light
Much, much more than mountains ever do

And she, like a ghost beside me
Goes down with the ease of a dolphin
And emerges unlearned, unshamed, unharmed
For she is the perfect creature, natural in every feature
And I am the geek with the alchemists' stone

The haunting melody filled the church, rising from the speakers strategically placed on the large, stone, arched, columns as the audience sat mesmerised by the powerful sound emanating from someone so fragile. Mary's mum closed her eyes and transported herself back to her living room, listening as her daughter sang to her dad at bedtime. She didn't want to open them, for it to end. Billy wouldn't be walking into the living room smiling, and cuddling up to his wife any minute.

For all of you who must discover
For all who seek to understand
For having left the path of others
You'll find a very special hand

. . .

And it is a holy thing
  And it is a precious time
  And it is the only way
  Forget-me-nots among the snow
  It's always been, and so it goes
  To ponder his death and his life eternally

For all of you who must discover
  For all who seek to understand
  For having left the path of others
  You'll find a very special hand

And it is a holy thing
  And it is a precious time
  And it is the only way
  Forget-me-nots among the snow
  It's always been, and so it goes
  To ponder his death and his life eternally

One bright blue rose outlives all those
  Two thousand years, and still it goes
  To ponder his death and his life eternally.

The church congregation was hushed as Mary finished and stood with her head bowed, they then erupted in spontaneous, deafening, applause. The audience realised they had witnessed a special talent, previously hidden but now promoted to a wider, welcoming audience.

Mairi-Clare hugged her friend. 'I knew you could do it. See, you are special – in a normal way.'

Mary relaxed and smiled broadly, having gained a small bit of the acceptance she craved.

Father Dan's high blood pressure receded slightly. He was relieved the Mass had ended with no more drama as he stood with the bishop and the children and shook hands with the departing guests.

'You're a really talented young lady, very gifted indeed. What a beautiful voice. I'm sure your family are really proud.'

'Thank you.' Mary responded, blushing. She was not expecting a comment from the model woman who she had stared at and studied throughout the performance.

Chapter Fifteen

'QUITE A REGULAR HERE now, Mr Lynch. You must be well up the legal-aid table.' DS Lawrie laughed, sarcastically.

'Can we get on with it, please? I'm sure we would all like to be elsewhere.' Cal responded flippantly.

Cal's phone had rung just as he was leaving the flat to meet Suzie. She was always so understanding when he cancelled. He had fallen for her and even mentioned the romance to his mother in a letter; maybe one day, all going well, they would pay a visit to London. His mother would like her, though he hadn't mentioned the unfortunate connection with the past.

'As you wish. My name is Detective Sergeant Frank Lawrie. Can you confirm your name for me?'

'Sebastian Bradshaw-Collins,' the man responded in a low, slurred, voice, his chin held high to reveal a wrinkled neck.

'Mr Bradshaw-Collins, you have been detained for questioning under the Criminal Justice Scotland Act 1980. You were in Moss St, Paisley, and at around 5pm this evening you approached a female with the purpose of obtaining sexual services.'

'This is absolutely preposterous. I was merely in conversation with the young lady.' Sebastian reeked of whisky, his stale breath projecting across the table and his glazed eyes confirmed that he had been drinking heavily that day. He was very well presented, with a manicured beard and an expensive wool suit complemented by a silk, gold, cravat.

'Do you know who I am? Do you have you any idea?'

Lawrie leaned forward, his elbows resting on the table as he glanced at Cal. 'Surprisingly enough, no, I don't. Please tell me, Ah'm dying to know.'

'I am Sebastian Bradshaw-Collins. Named after my great grandfather, Ronald Bradshaw, 6th Inniskilling Dragoons who fought the Russians at the Charge of the Light Brigade.'

'That went well, then.'

'I am the conductor of the Sheldonian Philharmonic Orchestra, the finest in England. I have travelled the world, directed some of the greatest music ensembles and now a parvenu like you makes such a ghastly accusation. I am appalled.'

'Sebastian, you approached a female and sought sexual favours in return for cash. The individual happened to be one of my undercover officers. This was made aware to you at the time but clearly, judging by your condition, you didn't retain that information.'

'I admit I may have taken some light libations.' Sebastian swayed in the chair and saliva dripped from his large lips, though his Etonian accent remained intact. 'I am merely in this God-forsaken town to reconnoitre the area before performing here next week. I'm bringing the master, Tchaikovsky, to the masses and I...'

'Very good, Mr Bradshaw-Collins. You can have a night sleeping in our five-star accommodation. One of our butlers will provide you with a thick mattress and silk sheets. You'll be charged in the morning when you're sober enough to understand why.'

Cal signalled to Lawrie. 'Won't be a minute, Sebastian. I just have to speak to the detective outside.'

Lawrie leaned against the grey, concrete wall, hands in pockets.

'This better be good, Cal. I've missed my boy's birthday party for that posh prick.'

Cal folded his arms and bowed his head to the floor as he spoke in a hushed tone. It was a submissive tactic he'd used successfully on numerous occasions; it allowed the other person to feel superior while Cal always had the end game in mind and could offer a solution.

'Remember when you charged your pal, John Faulds, with multiple reset and housebreaking? You said you were sick of chasing him about the streets and wished he'd chosen a different path.'

'Not really the words I recall about that wee gobshite, but carry on.'

'This Sebastian runs an orchestra, right? There's a group of kids from the West End learning orchestral instruments hoping one day to be good enough to travel the world. What if we cut a deal with the conductor? Use his predicament to give the young ones a break, maybe get lessons off the musicians when they're in town. The deal being you let him off with a caution. If not, I'll insist your operation was entrapment.' Cal raised his eyes slowly, expecting a mouth full of abuse.

'Entrapment, my hole. You can be a right smart arse sometimes, ye know that? But on reflection, that sounds fine with me. You can tell Posh Boy the news. If he rejects it, he'll be charged and I'll make sure the press get his name and know all about his pervy activities. He's still on a night's lie in. I'm away to eat some birthday cake. The sarge will sort you out.'

With Sebastian safely tucked up in his cell for the evening, Cal signed out. He checked his watch and headed hurriedly for the door; there was still time to take Suzie for that meal.

'Mr Lynch?'

Cal glanced over his shoulder to see a small blonde female perched over the high reception desk, her hands clasped together and her piercing blue eyes fixed on his.

'Cal Lynch, Eddie Quinn's brief?'

'Yes, how can I help,' he asked, intrigued.

'I'd go home and get an hour's shut-eye if I were you, maybe leave Suzie for another night. Mr Quinn has been brought in to assist us with enquiries. We will be commencing interviews with him and a whole host of others shortly, and no doubt, he'll phone you to attend on his behalf.' The well-dressed woman smiled, swiftly turned and disappeared behind the door.

With feigned surprise, Cal looked at Sergeant Telfer who was nervously tidying papers on the desk.

Chapter Sixteen

McGURN SAT IN HIS boss's chair drawing on a roll-up, the smoke nipping his eyes as he spoke on the phone. 'Right, right, aye, aw right, okay. Straight away, no problem, aye.'

The salubrious room was now looking very sparse. The police had raided the office and stripped the place bare. The antique furniture and the tattered book sitting on Quinn's desk were the last remnants of the epicentre of the businessman's empire.

McGurn and Nails had spent the previous evening and early morning reconnoitring the various outlets and contacts to gauge the scale of the raid. It was standard procedure when any associate was lifted or a business targeted by the law, though on this occasion things were edgier as the boss had been taken.

'There's a tout. They want us tae pinpoint who it is,' he said, nudging his head towards the phone. 'And quick.'

'Ah've got ma suspects,' replied Nails, frowning maliciously.

'Everything's shut down 'til we're ordered different. Nae movement. Cops know too much, they think. Lifted too many people for it jist tae piss the boss off.'

* * *

Cal had dropped in on Suzie to pass on the news. Her continual questioning had unsettled him slightly. You'd have thought she actually cared about her estranged father as the interrogative bombardment went on for what seemed like an eternity.

'Was it just him? What did they say? The other businesses – how many? How many police? Local police?' It highlighted even more her empathic nature, he thought.

Cal had received the phone call to attend Stewart Street Police Station in Glasgow at 7pm. This was an added dimension to what promised to be an intriguing session. Either they thought Mill Street was too close to Quinn's area of operation and riddled with his people, or they felt he was a security risk. Maybe it was manipulation of the media once it was leaked – 'Look, this case is different. We had to hold him elsewhere. He's a big fish.'

Cal met McGurn at 6pm in the greasy spoon adjacent to Gilmour Street train station. The enforcer greedily scoffed a full Scottish breakfast as he talked, mouth full or empty, which almost made Cal throw up as he sipped on a cup of lukewarm instant coffee.

'They took the lot – files, letters, papers, phone numbers, inland revenue shite, accounts, even the fuckin' photies aff the walls.'

Cal wrote as he spoke, not interrupting the flow. McGurn clearly had experience of debriefs given the level of detail and description he was able to offer.

'Ten uniform, five of them carrying short arms, another six in civvies and two fuckin riot vans sitting on the street. All in bulletproof vests, led by a wee blonde English bitch – sorry, nae offence but you know what Ah mean. No' seen her before. They were very cocky, confident. Mr Quinn said fuck all, just said tae call you when the time was right.'

Cal looked up. 'Why were you not taken in? Just you and the big reception fella left standing?'

McGurn smirked. 'That's easy, they'll be looking at a time when I was on remand, Ah reckon. As for Nails, if they've done their home-work they'll know he's as thick as fuck and wouldn't be part of anything, if you know what I mean. Mr Quinn trusts his judgement, likes having him around. That's why he's here, and that's all that matters.'

Cal chewed on his fountain pen as he processed the information. 'What do you mean, Franny – they seemed, confident?'

McGurn stopped eating and looked directly at him, his stony eyes making Cal shiver involuntarily.

'Look, oor office had been turned over before for fuck all, just harassment. Today was different. They knew wit they were looking for, Ah'm tellin ye. Invoice and payment files hoovered straight away, and the pictures, then oot the door. Everything else they lifted when they came tae it. Once they had awe they things, the wee blonde bird and her big-nosed skinny sidekick were all smiles, more relaxed and cocky as fuck. Mr Quinn was scooped there and then. She radioed, must have been the nod 'tae raid the taxi office. Pulling cabs aff the road they were, turning the site security head office over. Think aboot twenty-six bodies pulled in total, so big operation fur them.'

Cal glanced at his watch. 'Okay, that's all very helpful. Stay in touch. I'm going to Stewart Street now. I can't represent everyone, but let me know where they're all being held.'

'Nae bother, maist will be oot by the morning. You just make sure the boss is one of them, understand?' he hissed in Cal's ear menacingly.

Cal made his way to the Stewart Street front desk. The building resembled every other soulless station he had visited: prefabricated dull concrete, blue signage and plastic Formica seats ingrained with visitors' initials and burned with cigarettes.

'Take a seat. They'll be with you in a minute sir.' Another familiar feature: the rotund, ageing desk sergeant counting the days until retirement.

'Mr Lynch, good evening. This way, please.'

Cal raised his head from his notes to see a blonde woman standing with her back to the door, smiling as their eyes met.

'DCI Nicki Henshaw, Serious Crime Squad.' She stretched out her hand, her firm grip catching Cal by surprise.

'I'm sure this could have been conducted in Paisley,' he responded abruptly, glancing quickly at her body. She looked very trim and clearly took care of herself. The fitted suit jacket was struggling to hide the shoulder holster and automatic handgun.

'We decide where and when, Mr Lynch.'

'I will be meeting my client prior to any interview,' he remarked, making his way down the narrow corridor. It was an early marker, something he'd used on previous occasions to dictate the flow of the process.

'Of course you will. Straight down the corridor, last door on the right. Your man is waiting for you.'

Her accent was south London, Cal thought. He turned to face her. 'You mentioned Suzie McGrath at Mill Street earlier. Care to expand? Have you been following me?'

'Mr Lynch, do you think I'm paid to look good and flutter my lashes to show off these lovely blue fucking eyes? I know everything about your client, his estranged daughter and you,' she added tellingly. 'So please, no feigned surprise. You've got ten minutes, then we start.'

Quinn raised his hand as Cal entered the sparse interview room. He was sitting calmly at the table in an open-neck shirt, his sleeves rolled up neatly to his elbows exposing his thick forearms. 'Nice way to spend your Friday evening, Mr Lynch. Please make yourself at home,' he said despondently, pointing towards the plastic chair. 'Quite a wee show they put on. You spoke to Francis?'

'Yes, he gave me chapter and verse on the raids across your business portfolio. Have they spoken to you?'

'Who the cops? They know the craic. I wouldn't say a word without a brief.' Quinn tapped his thick fingers impatiently on the table, his eyes on firmly on his lawyer. 'So you're about to tell me you have a plan to get me out a' here?'

Cal opened his leather case and read over the notes from his earlier meeting. 'We'll listen to their allegations. I'll provide a written statement which you will read out. After which you do not answer any further questions,' he said firmly.

'Well, let's see what they throw at me. I might want some fun with them – make up for being stuck in this dump.'

'Anything you'd like to share with me. Why the raid on all your business interests by the Serious Crime Squad?' Cal asked almost dismissively, still mulling over his paperwork.

Quinn started to circle the room, stretching his arms above his head and tidying his appearance in the large smoked-glass window. 'Must be chasing somebody big down south and my name's popped up. They've done a history check and they've decided to turn me over.' He shrugged his shoulders.

Cal gripped his pen and looked directly at Quinn. 'Tell me about your history, then. That may help with how this will go.'

Quinn sneered. 'C'mon, you saying you've no' been nosey? Hate these places. Been questioned in every shithole in the West of Scotland and never found guilty of anything.'

Cal recalled Dixie's remarks about the network Quinn had in place – police, judiciary, paid council officers and criminals providing him with information and ensuring he stayed two steps ahead of the law.

'Granted, I was a bad boy in my youth but I'm legit. All my businesses are legit,' Quinn stressed.

Cal pressed again, hoping for a glimpse of Quinn's past. 'Your preceding years – why would they be interested? Were you involved in any rackets, anything serious, assaults? It may help me build a picture.'

'Nothing that Serious Crime Squad should be interested in. I was a bit like Francis, aggressive, determined, think later.' Still walking the room, Quinn's hands motioned with every step.

'So no cases, no trials?' Cal held his voice level while inside he could feel his emotions rising.

Quinn stopped pacing and placed his hands on the table, leaning towards him. 'There was one,' he said slowly. 'As I told you ... never guilty.'

'Mr Quinn, take a seat. We'll get started.' DCI Henshaw walked briskly to the table, sat down and was joined by her colleague, the big-nosed one McGurn had described earlier. Henshaw looked over the paper file in silence as her colleague organised his pens and notepad.

'So, Mr Quinn. I'm Detective Chief Inspector Henshaw and this is my colleague, Detective Sergeant Miller. We're both from the Serious Crime Squad. You've been brought in to help us with our enquiries into a number of serious matters.' She closed the file, lifted her head and looked directly at Quinn, slowly glanced at Cal and returned her glare to Quinn. 'So, Eddie – can I call you Eddie?'

Quinn nodded, leaning forward in the chair his face within touching distance of his focused interrogator. He had been in a similar situation on many occasions previously and was experienced with the routine which they usually followed. This latest adversity was a challenge but nothing he was overly concerned about.

'I've spent a lot of taxpayer's money watching you for the last eighteen months. You're good, elusive, very slippery. You cover your tracks very well.'

'Whit a waste, I hope ye have to pay it all back,' Quinn sniggered, maintaining eye contact.

'Oh, not to worry, there's always an Achilles heel isn't there. Once I found that I knew I could sleep easy.' Henshaw was looking to put Quinn on the back foot from the outset, unnerve him with her confidence and what may be coming his way during the course of his interrogation.

'DCI Henshaw, my client has been in your custody for nearly five hours. You have prevented him going about his lawful business and done untold damage to his reputation, for which we will be seeking recompense. I've already seen headlines in the *Glasgow Evening Times* as I left Central Station. I wonder how they managed to get the news of Mr Quinn's detention so quickly?' Cal was positioning himself well as the purported legal protector of his client.

'Bloody journalists, Mr Lynch. It never came from my office. But hey, Eddie here is a big fish in these parts. Isn't that right Eddie?' Henshaw clasped her hands and again looked directly at Quinn. 'Okay, so as you know we removed the accounts for four of your businesses. Err, let's see,' she stalled looking at her file, 'A-Security, A-Cabs, A-Construction and A-Holidays. Quite a nice empire you have, Eddie.'

'Amazing what hard work does for ye. Try it sometime,' Quinn snapped back, sarcastically.

'So, we believe what we'll find in your books is a web of transactions, cash being moved from each arm, large deposits from surprisingly average outlays.'

'DCI, this is very interesting but it does not justify the level of intrusion for my client and being held for so long in your custody,' Cal objected.

Henshaw continued to glare at Quinn while responding sharply to Cal's interruption. 'I've twenty-four hours, Mr Lynch, as you know. And if I go for an extension I'll get it. We're here for the long haul, so get comfortable.'

She stood up and put her hands in her trouser pockets as she slowly walked towards the large smoked-glass mirror. She leaned her back against the wall and faced the table. 'You see, Eddie, we've got your accountant telling us he cooked the books on your say so. But that's not enough to put you away is it?' she said, almost in a whisper. She tapped her knuckles on the glass. 'We have my good friend Margaretta Pisano at Interpol very interested in our Eddie, and telling us they believe you're heavily involved in organised crime. Say hello, Margaretta.'

A gentle knock came from behind the glass.

'She's very much a lady, unless she's on the grappa.' Henshaw laughed and waved. 'But Eddie, you're good, very good in fact. So all that wasn't enough. We needed the Achilles heel, didn't we?'

Returning to the chair, she opened her file again. 'For the record, DS Miller, I'm showing Mr Quinn items P1, P2, P3, and P4. Do you recognise these pictures?'

Quinn laughed noisily and nudged Cal with his elbow. 'You looking at this? Jeezo, blondie, I hope you have something better than this pish. I was hoping to at least get an evening meal in here but it looks like me and Cal will be eating at my expense in that wee Italian across from Central. You seriously questioning me 'bout giving to charity?'

'Hmm. The pictures show your very generous donations to a pensioners' charity, an approved school and two local amateur football teams?' Henshaw enquired.

'Once you've made a bit, it's always good to give something back. What was the last good deed you done for folk – have a lie in?' Quinn snapped.

'I'll come back to these lovely photos. However, they tell me you've never been charged with an offence in what ... over twenty years? And were only charged once with murder when you were aged...' she paused, looking at her notes, 'eighteen ... found not proven after a very short trial with witnesses developing amnesia.'

Cal had warned his client to say nothing but he hoped the current line of questioning would play out.

'That wis a long time ago. Mibbae I was innocent, Henshaw,' Quinn barked, leaning back in the chair. 'Look, stop arsing about and get on with this – yer pissing me off now.'

'A young father chased and stabbed to death in a Glasgow tenement close and robbed of a couple of pounds. His lifeless body found at the back door. Trying to escape his assailant, the police notes say.' Henshaw tutted, shaking her head in disapproval.

Quinn moved agitatedly in the chair. 'Not guilty, for fuck's sake. How many times do your mob need to hear that? Not fucking guilty of killing that man.' He nodded at Cal, who seemed to be in a trance, seeking his intervention.

'DCI, you have yet to provide any basis for holding my client and we are now treating this as police intimidation. I instruct my client again not to answer any further questions,' Cal stated.

Henshaw dismissed his comments with a wave of her hand. 'These pictures, Eddie. Anything look familiar? Do you see a pattern here?' She pointed a manicured finger at the photographs.

'Aye, they're all looking very happy with the donation my company has given them.'

'Of course they are. Who wouldn't be happy receiving a new eighteen-seater minibus? Four brand new buses?' she asked.

'Over four fucking financial years,' Quinn responded, glancing towards the ceiling and rubbing his pale skin.

'Let's take a break,' Henshaw stated suddenly. Miller glanced at his boss in surprise. 'DS Miller, can you get our visitors a cup of our finest coffee? We'll reconvene in fifteen minutes.'

Miller followed his colleague along the corridor. 'Why the break? You had him rattled,' he whispered in frustration.

'Yep, but his wee brain will be doing somersaults wondering how much we know. And the lawyer will be pulling his hair out because his client can't hold his tongue. Have the TV and video in there when we go back in,' she responded confidently.

* * *

McGurn scribbled quickly onto the writing pad while his colleague Nails paced the floor.

'That's a right few hours they've had him in already. I thought he'd be oot by now.'

'Calm down, Nails. The sharp lawyer is with him. Look, this list of names – they've been let oot. Get them in. Find oot whit they said, whit they were asked and judge how shifty they are. Might be a tout among them. I'm expecting a phone call.' McGurn studied the notes within a black notebook. 'The boss left orders if he was scooped ... different stages of actions based on how long he's been in for questioning.'

Nails looked through the list of names as he continued to walk the office floor. 'Naw, Ah don't think any of them would open their mouths even if they knew anything. I'll get them in and rattle them anyway. Ah've got ma' own thoughts of who's been mouthing aff.'

'Need it done the night, mate. They'll be another batch out the morra.'

The noise of the ringing phone reverberated around the empty office. McGurn placed his thick finger on his lips bringing his colleague's walkabout to a halt. 'Yes... Stage two,' McGurn spoke quietly as he scanned the notebook. 'Okay, consider it done.'

'Whit now?' Nails was back to wearing out the carpet, chewing at his fingers as he went.

'Would you stop biting yer nails, ya manky fucker. We've tae book hotel rooms in Glasgow, cash, names of two hotels needed at different locations, as soon as. Don't know what the fuck that's about.'

Nails studied his nail cutting, sniffed it, and placed it with his collection in the small box he kept in his three-quarter-length leather jacket.

'Manky bastard,' McGurn muttered to himself.

'Who's making the phone calls?' Nails enquired.

'Eh?'

'The calls. Who is it? The boss is in the nick, so who's calling?'

'Must be the boss's boss. Fuck knows,' McGurn replied, shaking his head.

* * *

Quinn sipped on the tepid coffee, grimacing as the bitter taste of the thick mixture hit his tongue. The harsh fluorescent lighting was beginning to play havoc with his eyes and the blonde cop was getting under his skin.

'Please follow my advice, Mr Quinn, and answer no comment,' Cal said.

'They've nothing. Just a fishing trip, that's all. Told you Ah'm legit. Ah'm more worried about my businesses being shut down.' He rubbed his forehead anxiously.

Cal continued to scribble on his pad, planning for the next session and hoping for a weakness to emerge in the police case that he could utilise and build around in the weeks ahead. The DCI seemed very confident and in total control which unnerved him slightly, causing his mind to race as he tried to figure out her next move and, more importantly, his own.

Nicki Henshaw had spent the break going over Miller's notes, gathering her thoughts and receiving feedback from the colleagues who were observing proceedings through the two-way mirror. They had all felt Quinn was rattled and she was premature in cutting the interview short. Her experience had allowed her to plan every session and wait for triggers at various stages in the process. Once complete, she would have a strong case to proceed with either charges or nailed a confession.

Henshaw's youthful looks belied her thirty years as a dedicated officer. Having lost her marriage due to her obsession with cracking cases aligned with her reluctance to settle down and start a family, meant more time dedicated to putting people behind bars. She had been transferred to Serious Crime after six years undercover in London, where she'd gathered evidence, infiltrated and set up anarchist, left-wing environmental protestors, drug barons and the National Front. Her clandestine career had ended abruptly after her real identity was compromised following a break-in at the Met and a price was put on her head. Now she worked in the shadows, but she was equally effective and dedicated to putting criminals behind bars.

She entered the room followed by DS Miller, who was pushing a large television, the wheels screeching with every movement. 'We ready to continue, Mr Quinn, Mr Lynch?' she enquired, glancing at both while standing over the table.

'Please. We want this cleared up as soon as possible,' Cal responded, lamely.

Henshaw continued walking slowly and leaned against the wall, looking at her file. Miller took his seat and fiddled with his tie while studying Cal's dapper appearance and preparing to take notes, setting out his various pens neatly in front of him.

'So where were we? Oh yes, you were telling us all about how innocent of any wrongdoing you've always been.' Henshaw smirked at Quinn, her eyes focused. 'I want to go back again. That murder you dodged, how did you manage that?'

Cal raised his head. He really should interject but he wanted to hear more.

'In the name of fuck, how many times do you have to be told? Not guilty.' Quinn's voice was raised, exasperated by the past being dragged up again.

'Not Proven, slight difference I'd say, Eddie. That unique option Scottish juries have.' She moved back towards the table and sat directly opposite Quinn, her arms folded across her chest as she leaned towards him. Her eyes darted at Cal.

'You see, I've been looking into that case. Family man waiting for a bus after a night out. An argument over a taxi ensues. A young thug chases him up a close and stabs him to death for a couple of pounds. He doesn't even rob him of all his cash. The guy's found a few hours later with multiple stab wounds and six one-pound notes, believed to be his Glasgow Fair holiday pay, stuffed in his mouth.'

Cal sipped the lukewarm water as he felt beads of sweat forming on his skin and running down his spine. His eyes were firmly on Henshaw but his mind drifted.

His mother had spent the day packing clothes in their two large wooden suitcases while Cal studied a book from the library all about the Isle of Arran. It was their first-ever holiday. Dad was due in any minute, having worked extra hours all month to pay for it. He needed a good rest, he said.

Cal had compiled a list of interesting places to visit and facts about the island. He couldn't decide whether to share them with his dad when he came home, or wait for their train journey from Central Station the next morning. Dad would no doubt be tired after a hard shift at the Beardmore Forge Iron works, but the train would be jammed and noisy with excited children running about.

'You see, I've a wee theory, Eddie. Your bosses ensured you would walk on that charge because they need a mad bastard like you to do their dirty work. And, because they kept you out of jail, you're owned. And here we are many years later and you're the kingpin. The top man,'

Quinn slammed the table and looked at Cal for support. 'In the name of Christ, Lynch, shut her up, will ye?'

'DCI Henshaw ... I' Cal stuttered. 'I will be submitting a written complaint to your superiors regarding my client's treatment. Either charge him or we leave. He has assisted you with your enquiries. You have a further – what – eight hours left to hold him? Which would clearly be futile, so please get to the point or we walk.'

Henshaw smirked at Cal and glanced at Miller, who opened a thick folder and flicked through the pages for what seemed like an eternity. 'Mr Quinn, I would like to take you through some documentation I have here. Evidence reference P5, P6, & P7,' he said in a soft low voice. His accent was from the south but less harsh than his colleague. His manner and his body language were also less aggressive.

'Mr Quinn, this account shows payment to A1 Holiday Bookings Ltd for a series of return bus trips for various organisations to travel to Spain. Would you concur?' Miller pointed Quinn towards the paper-work like a schoolteacher.

'Yes, that looks legit,' Quinn responded, welcoming the interaction with Miller.

'And err ... and this, Mr Quinn, the manifest from the boat cross-ings for the minibuses. This err... corresponds with the bookings, yes?'

'It looks that way, yes.'

'And all via the port of Dover, with two separate trips through Portsmouth. Mr Quinn, this other file I have here shows that A1 Secu-rities Ltd or A1 Cabs Ltd paid your other company for the fares of the groups. Would that be right?' Miller asked.

'Well, the groups would collect the money from their members and drop it in to the cab office or security hut and they'd pass it on. Simple.' Quinn shrugged, unsure where this was going. He'd helped numerous families, charities and clubs with generous donations over the years, and took pride in all the happy faces that adorned his office walls. Being seen as a legitimate, empathetic businessman was important to him to dispel the consistent rumours that persisted about his reputation and his interests.

'Mmm ...' Miller looked through the file, quietly talking to himself, his eyebrows rising with each page he turned. 'Mmm. I thought you might say that, Mr Quinn, so I prepared a route map. You will observe that all the groups involved, from where their respective treasurer resides, would walk past your A1 Holiday Booking Ltd offices to get to the cab office or security office.'

'I don't fuckin' know, do I? Ah own the businesses, Ah don't take the bookings,' Quinn responded, growing more agitated by the minute

'Were you, err, aware that your companies were booking the travel arrangements?' Miller asked, continuing to push his map under Quinn's nose.

'Nope.'

Henshaw untied her hair and wrapped the long blonde tresses round her fingers. 'So let's be clear for my sake. I'm a bit thicker than DS Miller here. You donated the minibuses to charity?'

'Aye.'

'You were providing them with the means to experience a different culture, to travel abroad?' Miller interjected, nodding.

'Aye.'

'You then paid for that travel abroad?' Henshaw asked, checking her hair for split ends.

'Naw, they did,' Quinn retorted, becoming increasingly irritated.

'Right, but you booked it … made all the arrangements. A bloody saint you are, Eddie.' Henshaw laughed, bowing sarcastically.

'Piss off.'

'DS Miller, play the video tape please. Evidence reference P8.'

The tape ran for more than forty minutes Cal stared transfixed at the screen while Quinn tried hard to hide the fear that was quickly being transmitted from his brain to his face. Fear of spending the next twenty years of his life in Barlinnie Prison or worse.

Henshaw broke the silence. 'So, Mr Quinn, what you have seen here is two of your *donated* minibuses, which DS Miller has pointed out your organisation paid for to travel to Spain on two separate occasions via the Calais to Dover ferry. While your driver and the lovely, grateful pensioners were upstairs on the boat, we were busy in the hold stripping the panels from the buses to check for drugs. We estimate the

126

street value of each haul to be in the region of £1.2 million. Unfortunately, we're a bit pissed we missed a further eight trips with schoolkids and football teams which the ferry manifests show took place over the past 12 months.' Henshaw clicked her tongue, shaking her head in disgust.

Quinn was thinking how he could escape this. *No matter how many times I used my skills and acumen to set up companies, provide jobs, create success stories, I'm pulled back down to their level.* He bit his lip, ready to tell all.

'I've told you I know nothing of this.' Quinn's dread was becoming apparent as he squirmed in his chair and wrung his hands in frustration.

'Bit lame, Eddie. DS Miller?' Henshaw said.

'Yes, Mr Quinn. In the first van, we marked the cargo. This in the main contained class A drugs, heroin and cocaine, with a small quantity of hashish. We replaced the panels and allowed the vehicle to continue on its journey. The second bus we seized in Dover a week later, which was last Thursday evening. The driver, a Mr – err – Grady, was arrested.' Miller smiled, the first time he had shown emotion.

'Yes, Mr Grady, Eddie.' Henshaw was back on her feet, straight backed and strutting around the room. She paused at the two-way mirror. 'He's been very helpful, provided lots of useful information to the team in there. He's wanting a deal. I'll probably give him it. Your networks in Spain and Morocco are being hit as we have this chat. The evidence we've amassed means you're fucked anyway, Eddie.'

Henshaw returned to the table and stood over Quinn who stared transfixed at the wall. She seemed to somehow dwarf him as he became more deflated with each revelation.

'See, we want everything, Eddie. You're the key to the warehouses, the distribution web across the UK, the money lending, the whole network, right down to the wee wannabe gangster who floods the housing schemes with your gear. And we've done that with some help from others. I can show the gear from that bus, *your* bus, arriving at one of *your* security yards, cut down and distributed via *your* taxi business to dealers in every scheme in and around Paisley and beyond. All chemically marked by our ingenious colleagues.'

Quinn lowered his head and clasped his hands tightly at the back of his head, looking uncharacteristically rattled.

Henshaw knew she was entering the final stages and her prize was in sight as he withered under the barrage of evidence. 'You're the head of the snake, and I'm so glad to have you here,' she hissed. 'So, Mr Lynch, I will not require the additional hours, thank you. Mr Quinn, you will be charged with drug trafficking, possession with intent to supply and money laundering. Our nerdy accountants are still going through your books. That's taking longer than expected though, looking on the bright side; I may get to add to your charge sheet. And we won't be granting bail.'

Quinn's veins were enlarging on his forehead as he smashed his fist on the table. 'It'll never stick, ya wee bitch. How many times? I'm a legitimate businessman!'

Henshaw sat motionless, eyeballing her fallen prey. 'Take him to be booked in, DS Miller. You'll be moved to Barlinnie tomorrow to appear at the high court on Monday.'

Cal intervened, trying to provide some reassurance to his client who was now breathing erratically. 'If the fiscal allows this to get as far as court, it will be laughed out. You've broken all manner of protocol. I require more time with my client.'

'Of course – once he's charged,' Henshaw replied, staring coldly at her adversary.

Chapter Seventeen

TUBBS SAT CROSS-LEGGED IN front of the large drum, polishing its bright casing with a chamois cloth. Mikey lay on the top bunk bed in the cramped room, while Mairi-Clare set up the record player.

'I told ye we'd be famous one day, didn't Ah, Billy Boy?'

'You've lost it, mate. That's a picture of some maddy on a white horse wae a big fuck-off sword. It's a drum.'

'Mikey, we're playing at the Toon Hall. How class is that?' Tubbs smiled towards Mairi-Clare, his red cheeks widening.

'Run this past me again. Some weirdo tells yer da's lawyer mate that we can play with his orchestra, just like that?' Mikey scanned his music sheet in frustration; his lack of ability, and the fact that his pal had stolen a march on him with Mairi-Clare, was making him angry. 'Tubbs, how many job forms have we filled out at that careers class thing in school?'

'Ach, hunners. Who cares 'bout that? We're heading for the big time here, mate. This guy's a conductor. Ah heard they always include young ones in every toon they play in, and they're playing oor song –

Capriccio Italien. And we've got two free front-row tickets each for the auld yins.'

Mikey jumped down from the bed, flute in hand. 'We're no' good enough. We'll make arses of ourselves.' His voice took on an uncharacteristically negative tone.

'Just keep practising. We'll go over the timings again until its second nature. Anyway, there'll be others playing instruments to cover all our mistakes. Try not to worry,' Mairi-Clare reassured him, placing the needle delicately on the Tchaikovsky LP.

She liked visiting Tubbs' house; it was constantly noisy and full of laughter. It allowed her to escape home, where her parents were at each other's throats frequently, primarily about the lack of money and job opportunities.

'You can use my tickets. My mum and dad are out that evening at a job fair,' she announced, lowering her head.

'That's a shame,' Tubbs said softly, placing his arm around her diminutive shoulders.

'Mikey, ma da says it's a lot of shite but ma maw is making him go, so you better tell yer auld man. Mairi, can wee Joe punt your free tickets seeing as he's no part of this?'

Mairi shrugged, while Tubbs struggled to hide his excitement. His eyes lit up as his smile grew wider. 'Right, Billy Boy, let's hear ye again. We've a big posh audience tae get ready for.'

Grace hummed and proudly smiled at herself in the mirror as she applied her make up. Seldom did she have the opportunity these days to get dressed up, and never had she had the chance to see one of her sons perform on stage. At the Town Hall, of all places. Terence was nervous, she thought, which he always showed with his constant laughing at inane situations, an inability to settle and over-enthusiasm.

Dixie arrived home from his shift and left the day's wage on the kitchen table. Grace glanced at the cash. 'You're paid short. Thought that wis a big job? You've been moaning long enough about it.'

'Aye it wis, but Ah used some of ma leftover paint from another job. So, Ah cut the price. The wummin's skint, Gracie. Ah seen in her food cupboards, feck all in them. There's naebody in the hoose working. Ah couldnae take any more.' He put his head under the kitchen tap to wash the dust off his weathered skin. 'Yer looking great, Gracie. What's for dinner?'

'Nothing. Sandwich in the fridge. Yer son's playing at the Town Hall tonight with an orchestra, remember.'

'How could Ah forget?'

Grace thought there wasn't a single person in the last week she hadn't told about Terence playing with a world-famous orchestra. 'Be pleased for him. He's on the stage at the Town Hall, for Christ's sake.'

Dixie looked around the room studiously. 'Something different 'bout here, what is it, Gracie?'

'Very observant of ye.'

'Where's the fuckin' lino? Did somebody break in and blag the fuckin' lino?' he exclaimed, his pitch becoming higher as he checked the window locks.

'Oh aye, that's what the junkies are trading in these days – second-hand lino,' Grace responded sarcastically, her eyes fixed on the small mirror on the kitchen table.

'You remember yer boy... *Shuffle*. Ah think his name is – asked you for money to buy lino for his *crew*?'

'Eh?'

'Breakdancing. He asked you for some extra pocket money.' She turned to face him.

'Stephen ripped up the lino?'

'Aye, took one of your Stanley knives to it. Quite neat, I'd say.'

'Jesus, where is he?' Dixie responded angrily.

'Doesn't matter where he is, you've nae time for that.'

'Ach, where's ma suit?' he responded in frustration, heading for the door.

'Hanging up.'

'Right, I'll go to the merchant's, get lino and lay it the morra morning. I'll change in the van; meet you at the Town Hall in half an hour.'

'Don't be late, Dixie. You'll not spoil this for me, whether you're there or not,' Grace shouted after him as he headed for the door.

Dixie returned, his black pinstriped suit hanging over his arm. 'I won't let ye down,' he whispered as he kissed his wife on the forehead. 'But he's dead when I get him, feckin' Shuffle.'

* * *

'I'm shitting it here, troops,' Tubbs whispered, tugging at the ill-fitting black suit jacket he'd borrowed from a neighbour as they stood backstage awaiting their call.

The orchestra were in full flow. Their playing had kept the audience captivated all night with renditions of Tchaikovsky's most famous compilations, including *The Marche Slave* and the enthralling *1812 Overture*.

'How the hell can we play with that mob? They're amazing,' Tubbs moaned.

The backstage was cold and bare in contrast with the heat from the audience and the orchestra, which swept towards them. Mairi-Clare slipped her hand into Tubbs and squeezed it reassuringly.

Tubbs' mind wandered to the previous evening when he was lying in bed staring at the dark ceiling, his younger brother out like a light lying above him in the bunkbed. His dad had crept quietly into the room accompanied by the smell of fresh paint. Sitting gently at the edge of the bed, he'd moved the thick curtain to allow the streetlight to shine on his boy's face.

'Ye awrite, son? Bit nervous for the morra?' he whispered.

Tubbs nodded.

'Ye do know I'm really chuffed yer doing this, son. Ma boy, playing in a fancy orchestra. I don't even know what that will look like. So Ah'm nervous for ye, wee man, in a very proud dad way.'

Tubbs looked towards his dad and suddenly relaxed.

'Wee bit of advice, son. See when Davie Provan plays for Celtic, takes aw the free kicks around the penalty box. See, Ah wis talking to ma pal, Robert McGoldrick, big Celtic fan, and he telt me the night before a game Provan runs free kicks over in his head, plays out the whole event. Imagines how he'll connect with the baw, where it will hit the net, the lot. That's how he scores so many – practice 'n' mind games. If you dae the same the morra night, after all your practice hitting that big drum, you'll knock them out. Trust me. And Ah'll be in the front row wae the biggest, proudest grin you'll ever see.'

Dixie rubbed his hands through Tubbs' hair then retreated silently towards the door.

'Da, I'll do that. Love you.'

'Love you too, Terence son. Don't tell yer ma, she'll think A've went soppy.' He winked, comfortable in the knowledge his sons were safe, warm, and knew he loved them dearly in his own awkward way.

'Tubbs, see that career class stuff we've been doing in school. They forms we've been filling oot.' Mikey stared ahead, leaning his head on the rough Artex wall. 'Did ye ever fill oot a form for an engineer's apprentice?'

'Fuck's sakes, mate, you still rattling oan bout that? We're gaun on stage.'

'Just cannae place it.'

'What?' Tubbs asked, frustrated.

Mikey turned to face his pal. 'Ah've an interview for a job at the navy base.'

'Good for you. Now think about yer timings,' Tubbs responded, pointing his drumstick towards the packed stage.

'Aye, but it's in Portsmouth. Don't even know whereabouts that is.'

'It's miles away, Ah think. Fuck's sake.'

'Is it? Ma da says the job's a shoo-in. He'll take me down next couple of weeks. If Ah get it, I'll be down six months before I'm back up, plus its four-year apprentice.'

'That's mental. Ah've been offered heehaw.'

'Think ma da had something to do with it. Don't know.'

A stagehand approached to signal two minutes. 'Wait for the intro,' he whispered, motioning towards the conductor.

'Good luck, boys. Remember; just let the flow of the music enter your mind and heart. The timings will take care of themselves.' Mairi-Clare smiled confidently, plucking the strings of her violin.

Sebastian Bradshaw-Collins rotated on the raised podium and faced his captive audience in the one-hundred-year-old building. Funded by a local entrepreneur and designed by the renowned William Henry Lynn, the auditorium had an imposing balcony that made it feel like the audience was sitting on top of the stage. Sebastian could almost feel their breath as they waited, eager for the next enthralling rendition. Sweat dripped onto the stage from his manicured beard as he wrapped a small embossed towel around his neck. His white, tailor-made shirt tail flapped untidily around his hips.

Raising his eyes to the balconies then returning them to the stalls silenced the crowd as they anticipated his words. 'As you are aware,' he announced in a booming voice, 'our fantastic Sheldonian Philharmonic Orchestra have been touring this beautiful country of ours. And wherever we play,' he bellowed, 'we provide opportunities for young musicians to join us on stage and experience the thrill, the exhilaration, and the downright elation of being part of an orchestra. Please welcome your young people to help us play the beautiful *Capriccio Italien* tonight– Michael, Mairi-Clare, and Terence.'

'Fuck's sake, good luck, troops.' Tubbs grimaced as he moved out onto the brightly lit stage, squeezing past the seated orchestra with his large bass drum, the image of King Billy out of place in such salubrious company. He could hear his mum screaming and clapping beneath them but the lights beaming into his eyes prevented him from picking out his family.

He nudged up beside the principal timpani, a small, clean-shaven man with a miniature ponytail that contrasted with his balding head.

'You will not be playing that *thing* in my percussion section. You will use *my* instruments,' he whispered apathetically, directing the young musician to the large bass set out beside him. His eyes wide and pointed chin aimed at the already nervous Tubbs.

'Listen, big man, Ah've been hitting Billy here for weeks. Ah've also been dreaming about how I'll hit it tonight, and now Ah will hit it or ma big mate the conductor over there will boot yer baws.' Tubbs returned the eyeballing.

The timpanist glanced at Sebastian, who shook his head. 'Follow my lead. How embarrassing.'

'Ah'm Terence. You?'

'Marcus,' he responded indifferently.

'Nice to meet ye Marcus.' *Manners cost nothing, ya prick*, he whispered to himself.

The male musicians looked resplendent in black evening suits and white bow ties. Tubbs and Mikey wore black ties borrowed from their dads' wardrobes, only used at funerals.

Sebastian continued to address the audience as the guest musicians found their seats. 'With *Capriccio Italien*, we will hear what the visitor Tchaikovsky thought of Rome when he arrived during a carnival. You will hear his gift of capturing a cacophony of sounds and blending them into the perfect ensemble.' Sebastian's gift for showmanship was clearly part of his persona.

Mairi-Clare walked confidently towards the string section, her curled blonde hair contrasting with her black evening gown. The concertmaster met her with a shake of the hand. 'You will be in first violin, okay?'

'No problem, thank you,' she replied, occupying the chair in the front row of the sixty-strong group of seasoned musicians that was laid out in an oval to allow the conductor a clear view of all the performers. 'Good luck, just follow my lead.'

'Is this where the woodwind people – err – go?' Mikey looked nervously at the blank, dull faces staring back at him. A flautist nodded his head towards an empty chair.

Sebastian turned to face his orchestra, reviewing the new incumbents with a frown.

* * *

'I knew that suit wouldn't fit, Terence,' Gracie laughed behind her hand. 'Have you seen Dixie, Peter? He's late again.' She glanced over her shoulder, hoping to see him dander down the aisle to the front row.

'Not like him eh? He passed me in the van earlier. He'll be here, don't worry. He's not shut up about this all week. How did you manage it, Cal, getting the weans in the orchestra?'

'Oh, just called in a favour. Suzie is late as well, Grace. They might be sitting in the Vatican drinking pints of Guinness.' Cal laughed.

'If they are, he's dead. Though Ah doubt yer girl would darken theat door of that place. Ah hope this camera works.' Grace looked at the small instamatic and fiddled with the buttons.

'Excuse me, excuse me, sorry.' Suzie arrived in a rush, her bright red coat sweeping behind her as she found her seat next to Cal.

'You've nearly missed the whole performance.'

'Not the best bit I hope, sweetness.' She kissed Cal on the lips, placed her long black hair into a tight bun, and breathed out in relief.

'Mini emergency,' she whispered, eyeing the orchestra. 'Salon got flooded by upstairs. I had to wait for the maintenance guys to show up.'

'Did you see my wayward husband?' Gracie asked.

'Dixie not here?' Suzie responded, surprised.

'As per with him,' Grace tutted.

Peter's mind was beginning to churn again. He'd been held by the police for five hours following the raid on the taxi firm and questioned about regular clients, fares, areas he travelled to, money he paid the firm to taxi. They'd let him go, advising him that they would be back to speak to him in a few days and not to make himself scarce.

Nails and McGurn were a different matter. They'd questioned him for a full day in a dark room, threatening him and seconds away from inflicting physical violence on several occasions. Who was he talking to? How many runs had he done? Whose names did he pass on? Why did he ask to be put on the hospital run then back on regulars? The same questions barked repeatedly, awaiting a slip-up. Then the ultimate: your good-looking boy and daughter will be slashed from ear to ear if we find out you've been touting.

He'd managed to convince them that he wasn't a tout, helped by the letter from the dole advising that his money had been cut – the reason why he was back on the regular runs and appearing legitimate by being registered to pay tax and national insurance contributions. *They were looking for a victim. God help whoever was in their crosshairs,* he thought.

A crescendo of bugles, a nod to the Italian cavalry, startled Grace as *Capriccio Italien* commenced.

The nervous teenagers had practised long and hard for this moment and the timings were etched in the minds. Mairi-Clare was first up on fifty-four seconds as the violins made their entry. Tubbs smiled as she followed the rhythm and swayed like a natural with the string section. He wanted to give her the thumbs up from his position to the rear of the ensemble, but thankfully disciplined himself at the last minute.

Mikey's section joined in at two minutes as the flutes led the wood-winds into a gentle introduction leading to a crescendo and receding into a low, soothing, harmony.

'They're really good,' Grace whispered to Cal.

'Don't be surprised.' Peter murmured, his stare fixed on the stage.

'Wait till Terence starts hitting that drum, the place will empty.' She laughed out loud.

Tubbs' section sat waiting for their cue, arms folded with the tedium. Tubbs swayed as he stood over his drum, sticks in hand, mentally playing every note. He followed the music, anticipating his moment. He lightly tapped the drum at five minutes and continued to flow with the music throughout the performance. He managed to catch Mairi-Clare's eye; she seemed to be mesmerised with the harmony, her head and upper body connected to the violin as it moved effortlessly, elegantly, as one with the music. She smiled quickly then returned her eyes to the sheet music.

The conductor's baton twirled in front of the musicians as he allowed them to bring an Italian carnival alive.

Mikey was wishing this was all over. He was moving the silver flute towards his mouth in time with the others but not attempting to play a note. His mind was on Portsmouth and leaving home.

Tubbs danced from foot to foot, swinging his hips as his big moment arrived. His new colleague was beginning to warm to his antics and passed him a handkerchief to wipe the sweat from his forehead. The performance drew to a close as Tubbs hammered his big drum in time with the string and woodwind sections.

The audience were out of their seats applauding as all three smiled and were hugged by their fellow musicians. The conductor summoned them to the front of the stage to take a bow.

'Ye can keep *Billy*, Marcus. Ma work here is done.' Tubbs shook his hand and returned the handkerchief to Marcus's breast pocket, much to the man's disgust. The lights went up and, for the first time, they could see the huge audience clearly and pick out familiar faces.

'That was amazing, unbelievable. How good was that?' Mairi-Clare gushed as she hugged her friends backstage.

'Absolutely the best thing I've ever done, man. I want to do it again. Pity ma da couldn't have been bothered to make it. Probably in the boozer.' Tubbs removed his oversized jacket to reveal a soaking white shirt.

'You might have missed him in the lights, pal.'

'Naw, Mikey, there's an empty seat next to ma maw. At least she enjoyed it – fucking mascara was running down her cheeks.'

Their discussions were interrupted by a visitor who came and stood amongst them, making them feel uncomfortable. 'Very well done. To appear on stage with such accomplished performers in front of such a large crowd with no formal training takes guts.' He spoke with an accent similar to their own, though his pronunciation was of a higher quality. 'Mr Lynch has told me your story and I'm intrigued to see how far you wish to go. I can help you fulfil your dreams. Let me introduce myself. John G Cooper, Principal of the Conservatoire of Berlin.' He handed each of them a business card. 'I'm originally from Royston, the Garngad in Glasgow. I was appointed to this post ten years ago.' He readjusted his black tie and ran his fingers through his wavy hair as the group studied his cards.

'You are lucky, I'm just back home for a funeral. When I heard about this evening's performance, I had to pop in. We offer twelve scholarships to young students across Europe each year. I have two scholarships still to be filled, and I'd like to offer them to you and you.'

The friends looked at each other in stunned amazement.

'You, my friend. The orchestra is not for you. An uncomfortable performance that highlights your lack of passion for the art. You two? I don't know yet if you have the necessary ability but you have enthusiasm, exuberance, and vitality. I can allow that to grow.'

'Aye, ye called that right, big man. Ah'm just here to support ma mates,' Mikey replied, handing his flute back to Mairi-Clare. 'Go for it, troops.'

'Speak to your families. I'll be here for another few days. I've put my hotel details on the cards. We can discuss it in more detail.'

'Err, cheers, thank you, Mr Cooper. Would we be going, like, abroad?' Tubbs asked, slowly.

'Berlin, Germany. And don't worry about the language. We're an international school, so English is the first language – though you will learn German.'

'Wow.'

'Thanks, Mr Cooper. We'll speak to our parents and come back to you in the next day or so,' Mairi-Clare intervened, taking control.

'I look forward to it. Goodbye.' He about-turned and waved over his shoulder, his leather-heeled shoes clicking on the cold concrete floor.

'Feckin' don't believe this! Told ye King Billy would make us famous.' Tubbs hugged his pals tightly.

'Go for it, Tubbs. I'm off tae Portsmouth. At least you two will be there together.' Mikey grinned, his mind again turning to the apprenticeship and how his life was changing at a pace his gut was telling him was unstoppable.

* * *

Father Dan raised himself to his feet as the bell rang, as scheduled, at 9pm, echoing throughout the large, sparse parochial house. He lifted the pack of sandwiches prepared by his housekeeper from the hall table to present them, as usual, to Jimmy the homeless soul who called round regularly. He always asked for money but left with food instead.

'Good evening, Jimmy. Here's your...'

'Awrite, Father, you've got to go to this address. Someone sent me to tell you. They need your help.' A skinny youth stood in front of him, his facial features hidden behind a large scarf and a black skip cap pulled over his eyes. He handed over a folded piece of paper.

'Who are you, son? Remove that scarf immediately. You sound familiar, boy.'

'Can't do that, Father Dan. Just go to that address before ten o'clock,' the youth replied, walking swiftly towards the front gate.

'The reason, may I ask?' Father Dan called after him.

'Somebody's sick, I think. Needs your prayers. Good luck, Father.'

The priest's eyes followed the boy as he ran down the street into the blackness. Putting on his heavy coat and black trilby hat, he placed his stole, bible, and rosary in his pocket. He left the sandwiches and flask on the polished mosaic step, wrapped the woollen collar around his thick neck, and made his way out into the evening drizzle. A gentle wind seemed to match his own sighs.

Home visits were a bit of a rarity these days. Typically, he was called for the last rites at the local hospital, the odd serious car accident or drug overdose. The youth didn't seem unduly anxious – must be an old relation and the partner was panicking. Everyone wanted to speak to God when the time came.

The tenements of Tweed Street were in darkness as Father Dan squinted to read the scrap of paper under the orange streetlight that coloured the light rain as it fell. Fifty-nine Tweed Street. Steel shutters and doors covered the building.

'This can't be right,' he murmured to himself.

Only one close seemed to be inhabited, with a well-lit top-floor flat that looked occupied. He noticed the blinds twitching as someone observed his movements. *Ah, must be expecting me,* he thought as he crossed the street.

'Father, in here.' A deep voice came from behind a partially open steel shutter door. 'This way. You're needed here,' the man said urgently.

The priest moved tentatively towards the large male who was dressed in a blue boiler suit and hardhat. He was trying to keep his chin low and his eyes on the priest in between scanning up and down the deserted street.

As Father Dan entered the close, the dampness immediately caught on his nostrils and gathered in his throat. The man closed the large door noisily behind him. The entrance was dimly lit with small lights spread along cabling towards the stairs and the landing. The flats had been stripped of any value: copper pipes severed, previously gleaming tiles smashed into thousands of pieces, and house doors removed for resale.

'Up the stairs. Someone will meet you there.'

'What's going...?'

'Just go or it'll be too late,' the man hissed quietly, revealing his impatience.

Father Dan followed his instruction. *Builders' working so late in a derelict property was ridiculous,* he thought; *someone must have been injured.* A man stood on the stairs dressed in black, dominating the landing space, his face masked by a balaclava. He beckoned the priest up the remaining flight of stairs.

'What is the meaning of this?' Father Dan asked, trying to remain composed, placing his hands in his coat pockets to hide their shaking. The tall individual put his hand on the priest's elbow and walked him to a vacant property. The clatter of their footsteps on the bare floorboards reverberated around the shell of a building. The previous tenants' wallpaper was still visible, with the outline of family picture frames leaving their mark.

'Someone wants to speak to you, Father. He is, how should I say, helping us with our enquiries.'

'In the name of God, what in Heaven's name is going on here?' The priest attempted to wrestle himself free to make his escape.

'Sorry, you can't do that. This man needs you, and so do I.'

A man sat tied to a chair, stripped to the waist, his head bowed. His chest rising and falling was the only evidence of life. Another male stood threateningly in the corner, his off-white vest splattered with blood.

Father Dan knelt in front of the man on the chair and gently lifted his bloodied chin. His face was saturated with blood and one eye swollen, already turning purple. Although he seemed unconscious, his hands hanging loose from the thick rope tied around his forearms shook incessantly. Fingernails lay strewn on the bloodstained floor, ripped violently from their roots.

'In the name of God... Dixie,' Father Dan screamed in shock. 'What is the meaning of this? Untie this man immediately, he needs a doctor.'

The masked man lifted the priest under the armpits and pulled him to the entrance of what had been a bathroom. 'Father, Dixie here has information that I require. Now, if he doesn't provide it, I'm going to kill him,' he whispered menacingly. 'You may convince him to tell me what I need to know. You can hear his confession and then give him the last rites ... just in case.' A strong smell of cigarettes and stale beer came from his breath.

'Are you crazy? You'll never get away with this. I'll go straight to the police. This is...is utterly evil,' Father Dan stuttered.

'Listen, holy man, of course I'll get away with it. It's what I do. It's my job.' His smirk was visible through the mask as he lifted Dixie's head by the hair and tried to shake him awake.

Father Dan was beginning to take in his surroundings to observe what evidence he could. The accents weren't local – Liverpudlian, he thought. He could see a chipped tooth and a large Roman nose through the mask. The rope around Dixie's arms was commonly used by builders.

'And I don't think you'll be going near the bizzies. See, I may not come across as an avid Catholic but I know some things. I know that once you hear his confession, which you will, you won't want to fall foul of canon law and break the sacramental seal. *Latae sententiae?*'

The masked man tapped Dixie on the back of the head with a Browning pistol then cocked the gun and pushed it hard behind Dixie's ear.

'Hear his confession and give him the last rites. The lad will relax after that and we can all go home. I'll be in the hall. And don't try anything – the windows are shuttered.' He nodded to his colleague to follow him as Father Dan knelt in front of the unconscious Dixie. '*Sweeeet sacrament divine... Sweet sacrament divine.*' He mocked menacingly, as he moved toward the hallway.

'Dixie, Dixie Clark.' The Priest spoke softly as he wiped Dixie's face with an old handkerchief he'd found in his coat pocket. 'Dixie, it's me, Father Dan. Can you hear me, my friend? In the name of God, what have they done to you?'

Dixie raised his head slowly and stared confusedly at the priest. He scanned the room, realising he hadn't just woken from a bad dream. His predicament came flooding back and he began to panic, his body shaking as he tried to free his bound arms. The thick rope tearing at his skin. Blood continued to pour over his only functioning eye as Father Dan tried unsuccessfully to stem the flow with what cloth material he could find in his pockets.

'Dixie, its Dan. Father Dan. What's happened, son?'

Dixie let blood drip from his mouth. The congealed clot dropping onto his bare chest. 'Father, I don't know. They said I set up Quinn by speaking to the polis 'cause Ah worked in his office, heard stuff. Lot of shite, honest to God. You've got tae help me. Ah don't know what tae tell them. A've not done fuck all, sorry, Father.' He continued to shake as his tears mixed with his blood.

'Five minutes, holy man. I've got my work to do. Hurry it up' the masked man called, ominously.

'Father, Ah need to be at the Town Hall. Terence is playing in an orchestra. I promised him I'd be there. Imagine my boy in an orchestra.' He attempted to smile though he was clearly in pain. 'He'll be brilliant. I'm proud as fuck. Sorry Father.'

'Its okay, Dixie. Don't worry, I'll get you there, I promise.' Father Dan held Dixie's blood-covered hand. At first Dixie flinched with the pain but then he relaxed, which seemed to reduce his shaking.

'Dixie, would you like me to hear your confession and receive Holy Communion? Once we've done that, you can tell these thugs what you know – anything you know – and they'll let you go. He's told me this will then be all over.'

'Ah knew you'd save me, Father. All the hours spent fixing your wonky cupboards finally paid aff.' Dixie attempted to laugh. A mixture of snot and blood came from his nose and landed on the priest cheek.

Father Dan removed the white stole from his pocket, kissed the embroidered cross and placed it around his neck. 'In the name of the Father, the Son, and the Holy Spirit,' he recited, as he made the sign of the cross on his friend's, bloodied, forehead.

'Bless me, Father, for I have sinned. It has been ages since my last confession. These are my sins...' Dixie was slipping in and out of consciousness and was almost incoherent. 'Ah love my children with all my heart. Ah haven't given them all that they wanted, but Ah gave them everything ah had... And Gracie, Father, lovely Gracie...' He raised his head and opened his functioning eye as far as he could. 'Ah'm not getting out of this, am Ah, Father?'

Father Dan's eyes filled with tears, which ran down his cheeks and mixed with Dixie's on the stained floor. 'You're a beautiful man, Dixie Clark, but the good Lord isn't getting you just yet. We will say an Our Father and I will give you Holy Communion. Then please tell these people what you know, and I'll take you to the Town Hall to hear Terence play, okay?'

'Ye know, I think it's that idiot Nails. He never liked me since school. He's done this.'

'Our Father, Dixie.'

'Our Father, who art in heaven...'

Dixie fell unconscious again though he appeared more settled. He stopped shaking and his breathing returned to normal.

Father Dan placed the Holy Eucharist in his open mouth and wrapped his rosary around Dixie's swollen fingers. He removed his stole and wiped his parishioner's face clean of blood, using every inch of the sacred garment as tears blurred his vision.

Dixie's head slumped and his chin rested on his chest. Father Dan stood, kissed the stole, and placed it in his pocket. He faced the masked man. 'I'll wait at the bottom of the stairs and take him home when you're finished with your questions.' He spoke firmly, seeking out the dark eyes behind the mask.

'No you won't, holy man. You'll head home. You'll be followed, so don't go anywhere else. Your phone lines have been cut as a precaution. Go to the bizzies and you won't be able to provide such *solace* to those in need ever again.'

Father Dan placed his face directly in front of the masked man's, almost touching his large nose. 'I'll never hear your confession because you will burn in the fires of hell. I have preached every Sunday about evil, sometimes doubting myself. Now I know it really does exist. Thank you,' he whispered. He turned and looked at his friend, desperate to help him. 'Just as I know God is present in this room.'

'Get him out of here.'

Returning to the bathroom the masked man sat on the edge of the bath, placed the barrel of the gun ominously under Dixies chin, and raised his head forcibly from his bloodstained chest.

'Right Dixie Clark, this is what will happen. You'll tell me what you heard when working around my friend's office, agreed?'

Dixie slowly focused his thoughts. He was now settled and accepting whatever fate awaited him, continually reciting the Hail Mary repeatedly in his head. 'Aye, nae problem.' He whispered.

'And that new lawyer friend of yours.' He rubbed the gun menacingly from Dixie's swollen jaw to his bleeding template. 'You can tell me everything you know about him as well lad, can't you?'

'Aye, nae problem.'

'Good lad, Dixie Clark. We'll get this cleared up then, eh. Then we can put your shoes back on, get you cleaned up. Once we do that, we'll all calmly walk out of this dump and let you go, just up the street. You can walk home from there, lad. Does that sound like a plan, Dixie?'

Dixie was now controlling his breathing. He knew to engage his brain he had to ensure his thoughts were as clear as possible. Only his imagination, he thought would allow him to survive this situation and return safely to his loving family.

Feeling totally helpless, Father Dan hurried from the close and along the dimly lit street, glancing frantically behind him, looking for shadows. He was sure someone was watching him from the occupied house. There seemed to be figures at each corner he turned, darting in and out of the darkness, or watching him from static cars, tracking his every step. He made his way to his chapel and immediately knelt and prayed before the marble altar, his eyes fixed on the sacrifice of his Saviour hanging high above, forlornly, from the Cross. Clutching his bloodstained stole tightly he prayed for his friend, he prayed for the challenge of faith placed before him. He prayed for guidance to do the right thing.

Chapter Eighteen

THE SHRILL OF THE ringing phone disturbed the early-morning solitude of the office. This was Cal's favourite time of the day when he could gather his thoughts uninterrupted and plan for what lay ahead.

'Have you seen him, Cal? Ah'm getting a bit worried.'

'He'll be fine, Grace. He's probably been out with his pals, had too many beers, and fallen asleep. He'll be on his way home as we speak, with his tail between his legs.'

'Ah'm no' sure, Cal. He never stays oot, no' done that in years.' The stress was palpable coming from the other end of the phone. It began to frighten him.

'We've been up all night, me and Terence. See, he told Terence how much he was looking forward tae seeing him playing on stage, how proud he wis – then he disnae show.' Grace was crying quietly, clearly agitated with Dixies disappearance.

'He's a big boy, Grace; try not to worry too much. Look, I'll go round his usual haunts, ask around, and call you. Okay?'

Cal left a note on Ms Knox's desk: *Cancel my morning appointments, I have to go out.* He wouldn't settle until he knew of Dixie's whereabouts. He'd been warned that Quinn would be looking for informers once the raids kicked off but he knew Dixie, like most, only dealt in pub gossip. He wouldn't be part of the trawl.

The previous night had been a resounding success. The expressions on the faces of the three young musicians, accompanied by the tears of happiness from Grace and Peter, had made bending the rules for Sebastian Bradshaw-Collins all the more worthwhile. Suzie had hugged the parents with sheer happiness at what she had witnessed.

Quinn had been refused bail and was being held in the remand wing at Barlinnie Prison. His legitimate businesses were slowly getting back up and running, though a number of contracts had been terminated abruptly. Joyce's sources indicated that drug distribution was seriously curtailed and the network more or less shut down. All of this meant the search for the police source was the top priority for the gangster.

The trial diet would be in a matter of weeks. Cal would resubmit for bail, which would be opposed because of the seriousness of the charges and the flight risk. Remand would give Cal some thinking time about how he would work with the silk appointed for the high court.

The Vatican had just opened its doors for deliveries as he entered. The stout barman eyed him suspiciously as he stacked the pint glasses.

'It's okay, I'm not the police,' Cal said with a smile and a raised open palm.

'Ah know, yer Dixie's mate.' The man continued his work, his eyes on his visitor.

'It's him I'm after. Have you seen him, was he in last night?'

'Haud oan, I'll check.' The barman opened the till and lifted the tray, pulling out envelopes. 'Naw, he wasn't in. Three envelopes still here fur him. Folk will have left it for him for jobs he'd done. So naw, wisnae in.'

'Okay, here's my card. If he turns up, drunk or sober, call me, please. He's not in any bother.' Cal moved towards the double doors, the sun's early morning rays warming the stained-glass panels.

'Wait, wis last night no' his boy's concert thing?'

'The orchestra, yes.'

'Ah well, there's yer answer. Didnae shut up about that all week. He'd have been there. Said he couldnae wait tae see the wee man on stage. Try his house.'

'Oh, right. Thanks for that. Remember if you see him...'

'Call.'

Cal exited onto the dusty pavement, the swing door clipping his heels. Where would he check next? He realised that he knew very little about his so-called friend; he'd just used him for his own ends.

* * *

'Cal, you better come with me.' DS Lawrie was standing next to his car and motioned for Cal to join him inside it. The police radio crackled incessantly as the policeman took a deep draw from his cigarette while performing a U-turn. He sped up towards the West End Cross. 'Something you have to see.'

Lawrie brought the car to a gradual halt at the top of the brae overlooking Tweed Street. There was a hive of activity at the bottom of the hill. *Police Incident Do Not Enter* tape seemed to occupy a vast area and a plastic tent was being entered by individuals in sterile white suits.

'They've found a body. Bus driver spotted it at six this morning. I'm sorry Cal ... it's your pal, Dixie Clark.'

Cal looked at him in disbelief, trying to comprehend what he was hearing.

'He's not been formally identified, but the body had yer man's wallet and family pictures. He's been murdered Cal. Executed. A bullet to the back of the head. There are also signs of torture,' Lawrie said quietly.

Cal dropped his head into his hands, his thoughts frozen. Strangely, he began to recall the feelings he had experienced when he was told of his father's death – an emptiness coupled with a stillness where all seemed to be going in slow motion.

'I'm not involved yet. They've brought a Superintendent in from Glasgow. It's a gangland hit, Cal. Personally, I think they tortured him for information. After that, they let him think he was going home – had him walk away and put a bullet in the back of his head. Dirty bastards.'

They sat in silence, the only sound coming from the steady stream of police vans delivering uniformed officers to the scene.

'The guy in charge wants to talk to ye. I told him ye knew the family. Wants ye to go with him tae break the news. Cal? Cal?'

'Yeah, yeah, that's fine. Anything.'

Lawrie lit another cigarette and pointed his yellow-stained fingers at Cal. 'Ye know who set this up, don't ye? They're close to him. He's sending out a message. The two he bumped a while back were just never seen again. Now he's letting the community know who's in charge with this one – it's a fuckin' message.'

'Gossip doesn't help, Frank, it just scares people more. Stick to the evidence,' Cal responded, irritated.

'Okay, point taken. But the dugs on the street know who ordered this.' Lawrie pointed towards the unformed cop guarding the entrance to the scene. 'Introduce yerself to her. She'll send somebody to get the super. Ye know where Ah am if ye need me.' He squeezed Cal's forearm.

Cal walked slowly towards the cordon, his mind trying to play out the visit to Grace. He knew how the boys would feel, how they would react. That would help, at least. Dixie was no informer and, judging by the evidence case building against Quinn by Henshaw, more than one source was at work.

* * *

Grace sat on the hall floor next to the phone going through the address book. She had a bad feeling in her gut. Although she continued to slate their dad in front of the boys for being inconsiderate, she knew he hadn't spent a night away from them since the first born arrived. He worked hard but was always home, sober or paralytic, to stick his head in the boys' bedroom door and walk up the hall with a wide grin on his face.

'*What ye smiling about?*'

'*Nothing, just smiling.*'

The builders' merchants had seen him at 6pm; he had bought lino and was in a hurry, they said. The address book contacts wasn't flagging up any further sightings. He seemed to have disappeared off the face of the earth.

Terence sat next to his mother, the excitement of the previous night long since dissipated. 'Go and make a cup of tea, Mum. I'll call the rest.'

'Ah'm fine, son,' she replied softly, taking his hand in hers. 'Wait 'til he hears you're off tae Germany. He'll be over the moon.'

* * *

Terence's excitement, was tempered with disappointment as he realised that his Dad hadn't bothered to show up when they met the adults back stage at the after party. The teenagers stood in the corner as Sebastion held court, bombasting throughout the room, with local dignitaries listening to every word, as he constantly swapped his empty glass with the roving waiters seemingly endless supply of wines.

'I cannae believe it, Mum. Cannae believe, we can go tae Germany to learn this stuff properly. How did ye manage it, Mr Lynch?'

'Oh, my friend Cooper owed me a favour. Though, if he hadn't seen potential in you two there is not a chance he would have made such an offer. Very well done' Cal advised, shaking their hands firmly.

Gracie noticed a worried look coming over her son's face as he stared straight ahead. She knew he was turning questions over in his mind. 'What's up Terence, what's worrying ye?'

'It's Dad, what if he says no, what bout the money, how could we pay for aw the things ah would need?' he said discontentedly, the reality of the situation bringing him back to earth. *This dosnae happen tae folk like me*, he thought, *Mairi-Clare aye with her posh background, but no me.*

Peter grabbed Terence by the shoulders and looked directly into his eyes. 'Look wee man yer Da will be over the moon. I bet he'll be first in the queue at the post office the morra morning tae get ye a year's passport. And anyway what will you's two be daein' hinging aboot here – Mikey might be away as well, if he nails his interview.' He said, assuredly. 'Don't worry bout yer auld man son – he'll be beaming from ear to ear when he hears this news.'

'I'm sure he'll be super proud of you.' Suzie added, smiling widely. 'I'm sorry all, I really have to get back to the shop. You stay for more wine, Cal.' She kissed him gently on the lips. 'I'll call you tomorrow. Bye.'

* * *

A short, stocky male walked briskly towards the taped cordon, a colleague playing catch up behind him. Slowing, he studied the line of officers and their fingertip search of the wasteland as they desperately tried to find clues.

'Start the door-to-door as soon as. Call me in an hour with an update, if not before. Superintendent Irvine.' He introduced himself, removing his latex glove and firmly shaking Cal's hand.

'Cal Lynch. How can I be of help, superintendent?'

'Terrible business. You know the vic … the deceased?' Irvine enquired, stripping off his white paper overall. 'Not involved in organised crime. Clean living, I'm told.'

'Absolutely.'

'We won't get a formal ID for a while – forensics will be here for a couple of hours, at least. I need to speak to the guy's family. Heard you'd be best to accompany me.' He eyed Cal, his thick unkempt eyebrows lowering against the morning sun.

'I am friendly with the family, yes. Look, what happened here?' Cal asked, nervously.

'Good. Be there as their friend but also their lawyer – they'll need it. Let's go. We can talk more in the car.' Irvine quickly led the way to an awaiting unmarked vehicle.

He fiddled with his handheld radio for a moment in silence. He seemed very calm, efficient, authoritarian, Cal thought. Someone who'd been over the course before with similar incidents throughout his career.

'WPC Mathews here will accompany us as part of the family liaison team. Tell me more about the family. Anything I should know?'

'Nothing out of the ordinary. Three great kids, good parents. Nothing really. I don't know what to say,' Cal mumbled, still trying to process all that was occurring.

'You think it was anything to do with your client – what's his name, Quinn, picking off witnesses? Seems he's bang to rights, by all accounts.'

'I've no idea. Dixie wouldn't be caught up in anything like that. He was just an ordinary guy, worked, liked a pint. He's done maintenance work for Eddie Quinn, that's all. Why would this happen? Surely you have an idea?'

'Oh, various reasons. I've seen them all, believe me. But this one? Professional hit all over it, maybe linked to the heavy team from London and Interpol arriving to chase down the drug money,' Irvine responded confidently.

The car wound its way quickly through the West End and parked directly outside the weather-beaten sandstone tenement in Argyle Street.

'Mmm, interesting. Not too far from the scene. You ready for this, Mr Lynch? This is a break from our usual protocol but your pal Lawrie said you'd be of use.'

'I'm not sure I'm ready, but I'll be there for Grace and the boys. Dixie would do the same for me.'

Irvine pressed a button on his radio. 'Irvine to Sierra 2. Just at the vic's family residence. Let me know when the van is found and when that additional forensics support from Pitt Street arrives.'

'Affirmative, sir.'

'One thing before we go. Was he religious, the vic – sorry, Dixie?' Irvine asked.

'I believe he attended the chapel up the road there but he wasn't overly outward with it. Why?'

'He had a set of rosary beads wrapped round one of his busted hands. Some of the beads were embedded in his palm. They've been sent away to forensics but they looked an expensive set. Emeralds. You see him with them?'

'Not that I can recall.'

'Constable, have a car sent to the chapel. Get the Priest down to the morgue for the Last Rites. Find out if he knows the vic.'

'Yes Sir.' Mathews responded, immediately relaying the orders down her handset.

The close was silent being so early in the morning. The recently washed stairs smelled of bleach, which caught on Cal's throat. The white-painted gloss border gleamed as the winter sun beamed in through each large stair head window they passed.

Cal paused then tentatively knocked on the large oak door, fearing the reception waiting at the other side. Feeling cowardly, he lowered his head when he heard the mortis lock being turned frantically.

'Cal?'

He raised his head slowly, meeting the eyes of a new widow.

'Cal! Cal!'

'Grace, I'm so sor...'

Grace's words were barely intelligible and accompanied by a piercing cry. For a second Cal recalled his grandad's stories about the haunting keening of the banshee.

He caught Grace as her legs collapsed beneath her on the doorstep. He held her tightly, saying nothing, his tearful eyes finding her three young sons standing motionless at their mother's back. He signalled to Terence to come forward and they helped Grace to the living room. The two younger boys ran to their room, slamming the door shut, hoping to erect a barrier to the news they feared had come.

'Mrs Clark, I'm Superintendent Irvine.' His tone and speed of delivery were at odds with the business-like conversation he'd had with Cal just moments ago. 'I have to inform you that we've recovered the remains of a man this morning. Early indications and items on his possession suggest that it may be your husband.'

'No! No! Cal? Terence?' Grace grasped her son's hands and pulled him closer.

'We would require identification later today, Mrs Clark.'

'I'll dae it,' Terence intervened, his voice wavering.

'Terence, that would be really helpful but your mum or another adult has to do it,' Cal said quietly.

'Grace,' Irvine said, 'this is Becky. She's one of my team. She is here for you and the boys to help you through this terrible time.'

The WPC nodded in the background. 'I'll put the kettle on.'

Irvine bent down in front of Grace in an attempt to focus her attention. 'Grace, I have more than thirty serious crime detectives working to catch whoever is responsible for this – and I *will* catch them. But to help, I'd like to hold a press conference this afternoon. I'm keen to let the public know what has happened to your husband. Would you be able to do that?'

Grace sat up, her back rigid. She regulated her breathing and looked directly at Cal.

'I'll be with you, Grace,' he said. 'Do the talking if you wish.'

She wiped her eyes with her cardigan sleeve. She seemed to have aged dramatically in a matter of minutes. Then she nodded. 'Terence, call Peter and ask him to come up and sit with you and your brothers. I'm not having you left alone.'

'Becky will stay with the boys, Grace,' advised Irvine.

'Very good, but I don't know Becky. I know Peter. Shall we go, officer?'

The victim was still on site, Irvine thought, but time at the station before the morgue would provide the opportunity for some informal chat and help build a picture of Dixie's movements, lifestyle and contacts. Becky's role was twofold; she was specially trained to pick up snippets from relatives and feed them back to the investigation team; that was more important than providing tea and hugs.

* * *

Cal returned to his office emotionally drained. He had delivered the family pleas for information at the hastily arranged press conference. Grace had collapsed, her words incoherent.

An incident room had been set up and a freephone number and publicity posters showing Dixie's smiling, cheeky face were being hastily circulated, urging the public to come forward with information about this barbaric murder.

Cal felt increasingly agitated and helpless as the situation unravelled. The thought of the boys growing up without a father being there to guide them through life, share their successes and provide comfort when the inevitable disappointments arose, led him to a decisive decision.

'I'm heading out, Ms Knox. I should be back around 4pm. And put these posters front and centre on those windows, please.' Dropping the large sheets of paper on her desk, he walked briskly towards the door.

'Where will I advise you are?'

'Don't advise.'

Cal arrived unannounced for the visit. The forbidding high walls of Barlinnie Prison dwarfed his presence. Pleading an urgent need to meet with his client about the imminent bail hearing – and the strained look on his face – convinced the governor it was a serious matter.

Cal was still trying to recover from the press conference held a couple of hours earlier. Grace was inconsolable; she reminded him of his mother nearly twenty years ago with her dead eyes and an unfathomable pain compressing her body. She had no concept of the future; the here and now would last forever.

He paced the small, sterile visitors' room. Small panes of frosted glass in the grey walls provided little light or a view of the noisy exercise yard below. His anger was growing by the second, his mind fluctuating between his mother alone – still alone – in London and Grace.

'Mr Lynch, to what do I owe the pleasure?' Quinn still had a presence as he entered a room, though his appearance was now dishevelled, with unsightly facial hair and stained clothes conspicuously in contrast to his usual smart suits and gold cufflinks. He had protection on the remand wing from a local heavy who was employed to make sure he came to no harm from competitors or old enemies who wanted to settle scores.

Cal stared at him. 'Dixie Clark.' He stood close to Quinn as he waited for a response so he could assess his expression. 'You had him killed'.

'I like it. Straight to the point, Cal. Impressive.'

'Did you have him murdered? Three kids without a father. A whole family shattered and for what ... to protect your empire?'

'How many times? I'm a legitimate businessman. Ah'm tired of this. Ask me, Cal. Just ask.' Quinn was in his face, sneering.

'Dixie didn't know a thing about your business interests. He was too busy trying to keep his boys away from your smack.'

'Ah'm still your *client,* Cal. Yes?'

Cal nodded.

'Client confidentially, Cal?' Quinn whispered.

Cal nodded.

'Why don't you ask me, Cal? Just ask me.' He jabbed he finger repeatedly in Cal's chest. 'C'mon, ask me the question you really want an answer tae, Cal.'

'What?'

Quinn murmured under his breath, mocking with a quiet, menacing disdain.

Cal grabbed him by the throat and smashed him back against the concrete wall. Quinn was winded but he laughed as he struggled to free himself. Cal slammed his head forcibly, the noise reverberating around the sparse room.

'Wait, wait,' Quinn pleaded, gulping deep breaths.

Cal released his grip and moved to the other side of the room. He sat down and tried to regain his poise. The sweat was running down his back. *Back to the plan,* he thought. *Back to the plan.*

Quinn sat on the adjacent seat, his head lowered, deep in thought. 'Looks like the odds are stacked against me, eh? Mibbae I should cut a deal, get a reduced sentence.'

Cal rose from the seat and Quinn's eyes fixed on him, expecting further retribution.

'I was celebrating that night, just finished the first year of ma' business degree with flying colours. Ah wis totally buzzing. Already had a placement in London with a big conglomerate for ma' third year. The world ma oyster in aw that.'

Cal stood behind him leaning on the wall, awaiting further details.

'Ah wanted to go to the States once qualified, far enough away from the auld man and ma mad brother. But hey, the cops decided I wis the brains used to launder dirty money. And that wis it, career over. Spent ma days setting up poxy wee businesses and getting used by crooks and eventually ma rocket of a brother.'

Cal remained silent, trying to keep his mind clear of anger as Quinn opened up.

'I never killed yer da. Ah'd never been involved in drugs, violence, cleaning money. Been taken advantage off, used, turned a blind eye – fuck, aye. Client confidentiality, Cal.'

The silence in the room was filled by Quinn tapping on the table and the gruff verbal exchanges emanating from the inmates in the yard.

'There wis two of us there that night, me and Jim Junior, ma brother. We were trying to get two lassies up the road. He killed yer da for fuck all, the mad bastard. I was sent up for trial, knowing there wisnae enough to convict me.'

'Quite a story. It took you a while to share it.' Cal moved to face Quinn and leaned over the table to whisper purposefully in his ear. 'I came back to finish you. I trained long and hard for the moment where you'd be sent away for the rest of your days. Your empire obliterated and you left to die in prison.'

Quinn never flinched. His eyes were locked in a fixed stare at the table. 'Looks like someone beat ye to it, eh? I only ever wanted to be a successful businessman on ma own terms,' he replied. He was almost disconsolate in defeat. 'I won't win this one. Tell the lassie cop Ah'll tell her everything Ah know. Then you and me will part ways. She can get me another brief. Ah might get oot here before Ah die.'

He moved towards the large iron door, knocking his large gold signet ring to signal the end of the meeting. As he turned to face Cal, a new persona seemed to come over him as if he finally realised he was breaking free from his reputation and his secret life. 'I never killed your da, Cal. Ask Suzie, I'm sure she'll tell ye the full scoop. Bye, Cal. I dae hope ye get the peace ye need.'

Cal left the prison and sped west along the busy M8, his mind turning over with questions for Suzie. She was the girl he'd fallen for in a big way, who he trusted and loved. He was inspired by her kindness and humility, traits he hoped he could emulate. His mind would be focused by the time they met that evening.

The plan which had took so long to develop was gone now, wiped out. He wouldn't bring Quinn down from within by using his legal mind as he had thought. He would share what he knew with Lawrie and Henshaw. He had played a small part in Quinn's downfall by passing on the tip about the bus donations he'd spotted in the photographs in Quinn's office. At least that was a little piece in the jigsaw. No more secrets, no more pretence.

Fluorescent lights were still burning as he approached the office. A yellow glow emanated from the streetlights that permeated the gathering smog. Dixie's smiling face filled the glass windows of his office, as well as those of every shop unit in the block.

Ms Knox was still at her desk updating the diary, her hat and coat on ready for home. 'You're back,' she said abruptly, looking from under her small glasses.

'I thought you'd be gone. Not expecting overtime, are you.' He smiled.

Her eyes turned to the well-worn reception seats where a young girl in school uniform sat, blankly staring out of the window. Ms Knox passed Cal a note. 'She said she had to speak to you about the murder. Do you want me to stay?' she whispered.

'No, it's fine. Probably nothing. You get off home.'

'You sure? She's a minor. I gave her some of Jack's Coca Cola – he'd only be using it for his brandy.' Her demeanour told Cal a different story and that she was anxious to leave.

Ms Knox scurried towards the door, unhappy that her routine had been broken though she was visibly intrigued by the young visitor. Cal went to the seating area while reading the note. He sat down and smiled at the petit schoolgirl who was clutching her leather satchel while sipping from an old tea mug.

'Hi, Mary. I'm Cal. Ms Knox tells me you want to have a chat about my friend Dixie.'

Mary continued to gaze out of the window. 'I saw you on the telly when I came home from school. I see everything on that street. Nothing else to do. I saw you before at St Mary's.'

'Oh yes! How could I forget the young girl with the most amazing voice?'

'You were holding hands with the model lady,' she said, still gazing into the November darkness.

'Well, Miss McGrath could pass for a model, I suppose.'

'I seen them take that man in to the close then take him out again.' She pointed to the poster and turned to face Cal. 'I saw the priest, Father Dan. Is she your wife?'

Cal's could feel his heart thumping in his chest.

'They took him in from a wee blue van with lino on the roof. Then they took him out later, carried him at twelve o'clock, when the street was quiet. He was all bloody. I think he was crying.'

'Who took him, Mary?'

'Then you said on the telly he was dead, that man.'

'Can you remember who took him, Mary? What did they look like?' Cal pressed, trying to remain calm so as not to spook her.

'Three men, kind of hidden faces. I watched from my room,

nothing else to do. I've seen them for months, in and out of that close where Jessica Brogan used to stay. I hated that bitch. She used to call me names because I'm different.' Mary's jaw tightened as she recalled her encounters with her old neighbour. 'They can't see me, though, in my room.'

Cal studied the scrap of paper, pausing to stay calm. 'So you stay here Mary?'

Mary nodded. 'Number 59 is across the road. That's where they use.'

'Mary, it's great that you've come to speak to me. I'm going to make a quick call from my office and then I'll drive you home. Is that okay? I'm sure your mum and dad will be wondering where you are.'

'Just Mum. Dad's dead,' she said sharply.

Cal called Suzie's salon, knowing it was her night for working late.

'Can we go, Mr Lynch?' Mary shouted.

'I'll be with you in a tick, Mary. Just one more call.'

The line was answered. 'I need to see you...' He kicked the office door shut with his heel.

* * *

Cal brought the car to a halt in the deserted street, the only sign of life a cat's eyes reflecting in the headlights. 'Does anyone else live on the street, Mary?'

'Nope,' she replied. 'Council says to Mum they'll move us next week but they've being saying that every time she calls.'

Cal scanned the tall vacant buildings. The first two floors windows and doors were shrouded in metal grills and steel shutters; the remaining windows were bare, with old curtains fluttering through the broken glass.

'I have to go. Don't tell my mum I was round. That's the close over there.' Mary reached for the door handle and stepped out of the car. 'The model, is she your wife?'

'Miss McGrath? No, Mary. Why do you ask?'

'Mmm. She does have long, shiny black hair and a bright red coat, doesn't she?'

'She does. Is there something else on your mind you want to talk about?'

'Mmm... Black is the colour,' Mary slammed the door and ran in the close towards the stairs singing loudly to herself.

Cal walked towards the shuttered door; he would have a quick look to satisfy his curiosity. The door creaked free from its rigid bracket to reveal a dark passageway. Street light squeezed through the grating on the frames at the top of the derelict stairs. Slowly he made his way up the passageway, stepping through the rubble and broken glass strewn on the concrete floor. A yellow cable with small lights lined the route. A cold draught caught the stale dampness, making him pull his cashmere collar around his mouth and nose as he climbed the stairs.

The cable led to a first-floor flat. The doors had been removed, yet the remnants of family life were still present in what someone had previously called home. A clear pathway had been created through the builders' rubble and household items leading to a dimly lit bathroom.

'Jesus, she was right,' he murmured.

The worn linoleum floor was covered in dark pools of blood coagulated with grit and dirt. A wooden chair lay broken in a corner. The dirty-white enamel bath was half filled with stained red water and the mustard wall tiles showed splashes from where someone or something had been repeatedly plunged in the water.

He bent below the cracked sink spotting a piece of metal glistening in the dull light. Lifting the object he read the inscription: DC. It was Dixie's zippo – the lighter he used for his Capstan Full Strength. He loved to blow the smoke in Cal's face, knowing he hated the smell on his flashy clothes.

'You and yer fancy clothes will smell like us wan day,' Dixie would giggle, his laugh lines stretching across his face.

Standing, Cal felt a searing pain in the back of his head. His body tumbled to the floor and his forehead smashed against the toilet.

His sight was blurry as he began to come round. 'I'm dreaming,' he muttered.

A male voice laughed. A pair of glossy patent red high heels came into view and the sweet scent of a woman's perfume filled Cal's nostrils. He felt no pain; he was content for the dream to take its course.

'Why couldn't you keep your nose out, Cal?' The voice was clear and the smell familiar.

'Suzie,' he groaned.

'Yes, it's Suzie. It's over, Cal. No one interferes with the business.' She knelt at his side, her full lips beside his ear. 'Not even someone as beautiful as you. And to think I nearly loved you. What is it they say about keeping your enemies close?' She whispered, softly kissing his bloodied face.

'Tell me why.' He tried to lift his head but couldn't find the strength.

'Why Jimmy killed your dad? Why I allowed you into my life?' She wiped the blood from his eye, which was gradually closing into a swollen purple mass, with the back of her gloved hand. Her silky black hair brushed his skin. 'It seems your daddy had a big mouth. That was enough. Does that answer it? You should have just let that wee lassie walk home, Cal. Kept your nose out. You don't cross the line with the business.'

'We need to go, boss. Now,' a gruff voice interrupted. McGurn, definitely McGurn, Cal worked out from the aggressive tone. 'What ye want done?'

Suzie tidied Cal's coat across his chest and straightened his tie. He lay motionless, his one functioning eye seeking hers.

Slowly, purposefully, she walked away. 'Kill him. No trace,' she ordered without emotion.

Cal felt his feet being lifted off the ground. As he was dragged out of the bathroom door, the coarse rubble tore into his back and ripped his skin. His head bounced off the concrete steps.

His mind slowed even further. Almost tired, painless. He thought of his mother and smiled for his father. This must be what it felt like. His time had come.

'Armed police, put your hands in the air.'

Four masked men dressed in black ran up the stairs, their flashlights growing brighter by the second. Behind them, Lawrie kept close to the wall.

'Get oot through the other flat! Ah'll haud them up,' McGurn shouted to Suzie.

She took a final glance at Cal's body crumpled on the stairs then never looked back as she escaped via a concealed entrance into the adjacent tenement. Making her way out of the back door, she climbed into a transit van that had hurriedly been organised to be Cal's taxi to his execution.

'Get me out of here. Drive to the safe house. We'll head to Liverpool tonight then you'll get me out of the country.'

The big-nosed driver turned and smiled, his chipped tooth protruding over his lower lip.

'Don't worry, you'll be well paid. Move it,' Suzie barked as she lowered herself on to the floor of the van.

McGurn extended the time it took to complete his arrest by following the police instructions as slowly as he could. 'Don't shoot, don't shoot. Ah'm taking ma time so you bastards don't get spooked,' he shouted over the din of instructions. His eyes darted quickly between the two lead officers.

An officer placed his boot firmly on McGurn's back, his automatic rifle inches from the back of his head as a colleague applied cable ties to his wrists and ankles.

'Ye got me this time Lawrie, eh?' McGurn laughed loudly as he was dragged unceremoniously out of the tenement.

Lawrie had already pushed past his colleagues and was on his knees, probing for signs of life in Cal's limp body. As he gently held

Cal's head, dark red blood poured between his large fingers and saturated his suit trousers.

'Ambulance, now! Tweed Street,' he heard a colleague calmly order into his handset.

'Looks like I turned up too late for you, mate,' he whispered in frustration.

Chapter Nineteen

J OYCE REACHED INTO THE bottom drawer of his untidy desk and pulled out a fresh bottle of Jameson's and two crystal glasses. Clinking the glasses, he nodded for Ms Knox to follow him. Entering Cal's office, he placed the glasses on the table. The area was spotless and compulsively organised. The pristine vinyl records were still neatly stacked by genre on the old dresser.

He cracked open the whiskey and brought the neck of the bottle up to his nostrils, inhaling deeply to capture the aroma of peat from the ten-year-old malt.

Pouring two large measures, he turned slowly to Ms Knox and raised a glass in his thick fingers.

'Well, Ms Knox, here's to Mr Cal Lynch. An inspiring lawyer, loving son, a stimulating gaffer and now a hero.'

Ms Knox sipped tea sheepishly from her china cup, her head lowered and eyes fixed on the carpet. Her mind seemed to be elsewhere.

'Would you like to add a few words?' Joyce added, filling his mouth with the golden liquid.

The old chair creaked as usual. 'Leave her alone, Jack. But I will toast the fact I'm still breathing.' Cal slowly pushed himself up on his elbows towards the desk.

'Cheers, boss, and best of health. Sorry, no pun intended,' Jack sniggered.

Cal ran his hand along the side of his head. It was still protected by sterile dressings and the bruising on his face and neck remained prominent despite nine days spent recuperating in hospital. 'I suppose you never really know people, not really,' he mused to no one in particular. 'Quinn really does have spies everywhere.'

'Told ye that boss,' Joyce responded, pouring another large measure.

'Even within my own team it would seem.' Cal looked at them both.

Ms Knox broke the lengthy silence. 'Mr Lynch, I made you aware at the earliest opportunity of Mr Joyce's yen for lunchtimes spent in that pub which, as we know, is owned by your assailants...'

'Here, haud oan a minute, ya cantankerous auld get. Boss, she's talking nonsense. Ah've told naebdae, anything.' Joyce gulped from the glass and reached for the bottle.

'Jack, you're a bit of a hoarder in that desk of yours. You never throw things out do you?' Cal enquired. 'It's a good job I'm nosey. You mentioned it before the McGurn case but I never followed it up. Dixie told me about the Herald crosswords you do each lunchtime over a greasy pie and a pint.'

'That's right.'

Cal rose gingerly and stretched his back in an attempt to relieve the stiffness. 'But you're not that good at crosswords, are you, Jack? Bit of a mind block, is it? But you are good at listening and filling in the boxes with snippets and words that Quinn's henchman let slip in their semi-drunken conversations, aren't you?' He smiled, tapping Joyce affectionately on the back as he hobbled slowly between the pair.

'That's what reinforced the minibus connection – the scribbles you made about ferries, Spain, football trips. I joined it up with the photos on Quinn's wall and there you have it – the biggest drug-smuggling operation Scotland has ever witnessed.'

Joyce looked shocked and confused, unsure whether he was about to be sacked or promoted. 'Eh, right.' He lifted the bottle again then returned it to the table. 'I wouldn't sell you out.'

'Don't worry, Jack, I know you wouldn't.' Cal returned to his chair. 'Ms Knox, you never did replace this chair, even after I asked you several times. I suspect you didn't expect me to be here very long, did you?'

'I beg your pardon?' she responded, stunned.

Cal looked at her directly as he spun a newly bought Madness single in his hand. 'No one knew young Mary was here that night except you and me. But you called Suzie, didn't you? Passed on the wee one's details. They knew I would turn up at 59 Tweed Street.'

Ms Knox stood in silence, unmoving.

'I called in a favour. You have quite a large bank balance, with monthly pay ins to your husband's account originating from A1 Securities Ltd. Tut-tut, Anne. You could have hidden it better.'

Cal waved through the open door to a figure standing on the street. Returning his gaze to Ms Knox, he glared at her. Her hands were shaking and her teacup clinked in the saucer.

'I've already lined up your replacement. Lift your bag, leave everything else and get out of here. Jack, once you've lifted your jaw off the floor, escort this one from the premises.'

Ms Knox raised her head. 'Are you not interested in why, how I—'

'Not really. It'll be some tale of blackmail or a sob story.' He looked unswervingly at her. 'We could all take the easy route and enjoy the money. We could all just blank out the deception and hurt caused by our actions. But some, just some, of us still like to sleep peacefully at night. Anyway, this lecture is over. There's a police car sitting outside to take you to Mill Street where Superintendent Irvine is waiting for you. Get out. Once she leaves, Jack, show in your new colleague.'

Ms Knox could be heard sobbing as she lifted her bag and family photographs from her desk. Handing Jack her keys, she took a final glance around the office in which she'd worked for fifteen years, then she dropped her head and left.

'Jack, meet our new office manager.' Cal grimaced with pain as he greeted the new incumbent with a hug.

'You really don't have tae do this,' she responded quietly.

'Jack, I'm sure you remember Grace Clark.'

'Course I do. Yer boy used to rip me off for security money every week.' Jack laughed, breaking the tension.

'Grace, Jack here will show you to your desk. Just keep the diary up to date for the first couple weeks. We'll help you pick up the rest.' Grace followed Jack towards the main office. Cal called after them. 'Grace, Terence – how is he?'

'Away to Germany yesterday morning. Cried my eyes oot at the airport. Ah think that wee girl's ma thought I was an idiot. He'll be fine. It'll be the making of him. That's whit Ah'm telling myself, anyway.' Her hair was tied back tightly from her face, illuminating a shattered expression that Cal was determined to repair. 'Thanks for the money, by the way. Terence asked me to give you this album back. Ah think he's wore it out though, he played it that much.'

'The money wasn't mine, it was his dad's. He'd done work for me but never picked up the cash. Tchaikovsky, back in the collection – great.' He studied the cover like a long-lost friend.

'Not like him, eh? All change. His wee pal Mikey is away down south as well. Peter will miss him – he's away to some farm in Donegal and took his daughter with him, kicking and screaming by all accounts,' Grace responded, sadly.

Peter had retreated to Ireland after settling Mikey in Portsmouth. He was devastated by the role he'd played in the death of his childhood friend and sought solace in his spiritual home. He could not be around Grace or the boys because the guilt consumed him. Hopefully it would subside over time, though he was in no hurry to return to Scotland.

Grace had leaned on him during the initial dark days after the murder. The least he could do was organise the wake and work closely with Father Dan to ensure Dixie had the send-off he deserved. After the funeral he went on a four-day bender, only sobering up when it was time to board the train at Glasgow Central with Mikey for the nine-hour journey to his son's new life down south.

His information had allowed the drug squad to complete the circle and arrest fifteen local street-dealing networks that were being ferried around by A-Cabs on a regular basis. The taxi firm had lost its licence to operate and the remaining drivers were scurrying around looking for work elsewhere. They didn't have the inclination to decipher how the network had been smashed or who had played a part in its demise. He would keep an eye on any forthcoming trials, though Henshaw had assured him no roads would lead in his direction.

All areas were double-checked for future proofing and job application forms had also been implanted within St Saviours High office files indicating a paper trail for Mikey's apprenticeship via a local job broker who was now closed for business. The network of spies may have been rattled but no one was under the illusion that it had been smashed.

'Ye know Harry from the Vatican? He called me up. Dixie had some envelopes behind the bar for work he'd done for punters.' Grace laughed, tears falling from her cheeks. 'When I turned up, another thirty envelopes had been left by his friends. People are really decent, eh?'

'Because it was him, Grace. Dixie.'

'Cal, can I do this office up. It's a bit err ... howling.' She smiled, her eyes skirting the office as she made sweeping movements with her hands and forgot the last couple of weeks of hell for a moment.

'Of course you can.'

'Great, I'll get brochures. Ah'm thinking of a nice warm green, mixed with greys and some foliage. Okay?'

Cal spun his chair to face the Amstrad record player.

'You've a visitor boss,' Grace said, a moment later from the doorway.

Lawrie came in at her back, his tie hanging loosely around his neck as usual, the well-worn brown suit in need of a substitute. 'You're back, then?' he asked, lifting the Jameson's and pouring himself a small one into the used glass.

'Just about, Frank. Thanks for what you done, by the way.'

'Good job you phoned before you left the office or you'd be dead. Though you were meant to wait outside until we got there. A couple of minutes more and you'd have been a goner.' He frowned, shaking his head.

Cal sighed, flashbacks of that fateful night returning: Suzie's cold features and the steeliness in her eyes that was at odds with the loving, caring partner she'd been for the past few months. 'Any sign of Suzie?' he enquired.

Lawrie took a seat and rested his beaten, size ten brogues on the desk. 'No sightings. Henshaw is on it - she'll want a full statement from you in the next day or so. Tireless, that one. She'll chase her down. All ports are monitored and her details have been circulated to all cop shops and Interpol. Jimmy Junior was huckled from his plush villa by Spanish cops two days ago. He's been charged with drug trafficking in Spain, and word has it Serious Crime will push for extradition. We've a statement from young Mary which places the lovely Suzie at the scene on the night of Dixie's murder, plus forensics are all over that tenement. All that and your statement means...' Lawrie paused, taking a slow sip of the malt... 'she's well and truly fucked once she's caught. Ah cannae wait for that trial.'

Cal shook his head. 'Unbelievable. Now it makes sense why she was late for the concert. Then she sat there smiling and cheering on the kids with the poor guy's wife, knowing that she'd...' He sighed. 'One evil individual.'

'Aye, and another wee rumour circulating is that she is the mad brother's daughter not Eddie's. Imagine that. Anyway, not be long till McGrath is caught,' Lawrie advised confidently. He lit a cigarette, much to Cal's displeasure. Taking a long draw, he used the palm of his hand for an ashtray as he raised his eyes to study Cal. 'You heard about Quinn?'

'I did. Terrible, by the sounds of it.' Cal looked at the sleeve of the record, feigning interest in his adversary's demise.

'Knifed to death while on remand. Ye'd think he'd be safe in jail, wouldn't ye? Seemingly his paid security was stood down less than an hour after he had a secret meeting with the DCI. Not so secret, it would seem.' Lawrie sipped his whiskey. 'Chased him through a kitchen. He tried to get through a door but it was locked. Just like your da, all those years ago. Plunged fifteen times, just like your Da. In roughly the same places as your Da.' His eyes were fixed on Cal.

'Unbelievable.' Cal replied, placing the record down and feeling Lawrie's stare pierce him.

'Gets better, Cal.' Lawrie emptied the glass in one gulp and placed the cigarette and ash in it. 'He had six pound notes stuffed in his mouth. Which just happened to be what your poor old da, Peter Turner, had when Quinn or his brother murdered him in that close all those years ago when you were a wean.'

'I'm sure Quinn had lots of enemies, Frank. He indicated to me that his options were limited and he was considering turning state's evidence. I hope DCI Henshaw got a detailed statement from him. And it's on public record what happened to my father,' Cal retorted. 'And, believe it or not, I wasn't in jail so it wasn't me.' He laughed nervously and raised his hands in desperation.

* * *

'Take me tae yer Governor's office. I need to talk to someone. Right now.' Quinn barked to his warder escort, as he left Cal standing in the interview room of the prison.

He sat in the sparse office as he awaited confirmation of the meeting, the governor pacing nervously.

The radio handset broke the silence, 'That's them here boss, over.'

'Show them to my office immediately, no need to sign in.' He responded, in an apprehensive tone.

'Mr Quinn, we meet again. How nice.'

Quinn glanced up from the chair, he felt relaxed now, contented even with what he was about to do. 'Henshaw and sidekick, it's my pleasure. I've missed you guys.'

'So you want to talk, I hear.' Henshaw enquired, occupying the Governor's chair in eager anticipation of what she hoped would follow.

'I'll tell you the full scoop. Courier routes, names, businesses, money washing, protection, councillors, bent cops. The lot. I'll prove to you I wasn't involved in any of that shite. But I want a deal ... obviously.' Quinn smiled, as he rolled his large signet ring around his pinkie as he stretched out in the chair.

'Okay. We'll take it from here Governor, thank you so much for allowing us to use your office.' Henshaw glanced at the door.

'I want him gone from my remand wing immediately,' the governor responded assertively, 'I can't guarantee this guy's safety.'

Quinn laughed to himself.

'He will be, just give me a couple of days.' Henshaw pleaded.

The governor headed for the door as DC Millar set up a cassette recorder and Henshaw opened a bottle of water, passing a glass over to Quinn. 'So where shall we start, Eddie?'

'First, do you have the clout to give me a deal?'

Henshaw smiled over to her colleague as she played with the tall thin glass. 'You'll have a deal, if it leads to convictions. A reduced sentence in a secret location with a new I.D, untraceable.'

'That'll do me. Let's go back to the start then in the Gorbals, 1962. We can go from there. Time to unburden myself.' Quinn signed, almost in relief.

Henshaw and Millar had spent over four hours with Quinn going over all aspects of the criminal world he was a part of. Pizzas were sent for, toilets breaks factored in and a constant supply of coffee from the Governors secretary kept the information flowing. They left with the transcripts late in the evening with another meeting arranged for lunchtime the next day. This would give Henshaw the morning to sort the logistics of Quinn's extraction and re-homing to another jail, prior to any trial.

Henshaw received the phone call the next morning, "Don't bother coming to the jail, Quinn's been killed." One of the businesses *paid* warders had printed and sent out, to associates, a security camera image of the officers arriving at the reception area. The length of time they had spent in the prison with Quinn, and the secrecy surrounding their presence, had more or less sealed his fate. She wouldn't lose sleep over his loss. Her biggest challenge, she now faced, was using the tapes as evidence at any of the multiple trials she had anticipated.

* * *

'Not to worry, pal.' Lawrie smiled at Cal as he walked towards the door. 'Oh, I was speaking to another acquaintance of yours, Gordon McIntosh, the bent lawyer?'

'Name does not sound familiar, Frank.'

'Och, that kicking McGurn gave ye has affected your memory.' Lawrie went back to the desk and leant over it. 'He was the brief that had this place. Three years ago, he was jailed for smuggling gear into the clink and a bit of light embezzlement. Just got out of the prison on health grounds. He's fucked, full of morphine, and on the way out. He stays up north now, I've always had a soft spot for him. We kept in touch.'

'Right. You do have a soft spot, then,' Cal responded, worried.

'Said some guy fitting *your* description visited him in Greenock Prison at least twice about a year ago. This person had been writing to him around a *year* before that. Like a type of nosey, geeky pen pal. He was asking all sorts of queries about researching lawyer practices in Scotland, it would seem. The questions then moved swiftly on to Quinn and his business interests.' Lawrie stood, hands in pockets, awaiting a response.

'I'm a common-looking guy. I must have one of those faces.'

'And the intriguing thing is, McIntosh told this tall, smooth, good-looking, sharply-dressed young guy with a mongrel accent, all about

174

Suzie McGrath and her secret role as the boss of bosses. How she ran everything, took no prisoners. Mental, eh?'

'You couldn't make it up. When you find this young guy, let me know, will you?' Cal responded, cautiously.

'I won't find him, pal. I'd need to be looking to do that.' Lawrie reached out his hand. 'Take care, Cal. You hanging around?'

Cal placed the needle delicately on the vinyl and turned up the volume to its maximum. The trumpets of *Capriccio Italien* heralded the commencement of the carnival.

'I've only just got started.'

Acknowledgments

Thanks to Peter Keenan and Aine Harrington for their help and intuitive comments with early drafts. Jane Laiolo for her red pen and encouragement to push on and make it better.

Special thanks to Colm Donnelly for his creative input and cover design for a no doubt difficult client.

And thank you to Cara-Marie who insisted this whole project should be kicked off. For her support, enthusiasm, endurance and positive ranting over the last five years. It wouldn't have happened without you. Now it's your turn.

Printed in Great Britain
by Amazon

14064865R00108